Between Earth and Sky

Between Earth and Sky

Karen Osborn

William Morrow and Company, Inc.
New York

FIC
0815be

It is the policy of William Morrow and Company, Inc., and its imprints and affiliates, recognizing the importance of preserving what has been written, to print the books we publish on acid-free paper, and we exert our best efforts to that end.

Library of Congress Cataloging-in-Publication Data

Osborn, Karen.
    Between earth and sky / Karen Osborn.—1st ed.
        p.   cm.
    ISBN 0-688-14123-4
    I. Title.
PS3565.S385B47   1996
813'.54—dc20   95-10948
                                                                                        CIP

Printed in the United States of America

First Edition

1   2   3   4   5   6   7   8   9   10

BOOK DESIGN BY LINDA KOCUR

For Janet,
whose love of
New Mexico
made this book
possible,
and for my parents,
who gave me
the idea in the
first place

$\mathcal{A}cknowledgments$

I would like to thank Jane Gelfman for her continuing support of my work and her sense of vision, and Claire Wachtel for her numerous readings, her accurate eye, and her belief in the book that this would become.

Thank you also to the Kentucky Arts Council and the Kentucky Foundation for Women for their generuos grants; to Linda Osborn, Marcia Hurlow, Jeff Worley, Mike Jenkins, and Ken Osborn for their insight and encouragement; and to the following sources that helped me to learn about pioneer life and the Southwest:

Far from Home: Families of the Westward Journey, by Lillian Schlissel, Byrd Gibbons, and Elizabeth Hampsten; *The Lore of New Mexico*, by Marta Weigle and Peter White; *The Good Life: New Mexico Traditions and Food*, by Fabiola Cabeza de Baca Gilbert; *New Mexican Folklore of the Rio Abajo*, by Tibo J. Chavez;

Acknowledgments

Women and Indians on the Frontier, 1825–1915, by Glenda Riley; *Mollie: The Journal of Mollie Dorsey Sanford in Nebraska and Colorado Territories, 1857–1866* (Introduction by Donald F. Danker); *New Mexico: A History of Four Centuries,* by Warren A. Beck.

De la tierra al cielo no hay nada oculto.

Between earth and sky there are no secrets.

Between Earth and Sky

Prologue

The letters were there first, long before I was. They were given to me by my great-grandmother just before she died. Written by her mother, the great-great-grandmother I was named after, they were bound with ribbons gone thin as tissue paper and closed inside a wooden box. Unlike the rest of our family, which has stayed in Virginia, my great-great-grandmother lived most of her life in New Mexico, a place so foreign to all of us that the stories that evolved about her ended up sounding like fairy tales. My great-grandmother had grown up among cacti, Indians, horses, and mesas. She spoke more Spanish than English by the time she started school, and her younger brother and sister eventually disappeared like loose bits of sagebrush blown to some unknown part of the desert.

My great-great-grandmother's name was Abigail, while

I am called Abby. Beginning with the trip westward she took as a young woman with her husband and small children and ending years later when she grew old on her land in northern New Mexico, the letters were written to her sister, Maggie, who had stayed in Virginia. They followed the strange course of her life. After Maggie's death, my great-grandmother, Amy, inherited her mother's letters, and she did not think to give them to anyone but me, she said as I took the box from her. I was still a child, but she seemed to know the part they would eventually play in my own life.

I first saw Abigail's land late one afternoon after having driven the better part of four days, the letters only partially read in their box on the back seat of my car. I had quit my job at the university, where I had worked for ten years as an underpaid assistant librarian, and left my parents' house, a square colonial built to look like most of the others that lined the street of a large subdivision built on what used to be a farm. I'd grown tired of my life the past five years, the hours of cataloging books, the Saturday afternoons spent roaming the shopping mall with my sister and her kids, the nights I'd spent with one boyfriend or another.

Abigail's valley spread between two mountain ranges, with a river that ran along each side. While the mountains were desert-like, streaked with browns, reds, and yellows, the land between the rivers shimmered with alfalfa grass, fields of shiny pepper plants, and the paler green of cornstalks, which stretched as far back from the road as I could see. All along the roadside grew Mexican olive trees of soft grayish green, a luminous color with a hint of silver just beneath the surface.

The land that had been Abigail's stretched back from a gravel road next to a few old trailers. The address I had was still accurate, and I had contacted the local post office for directions. Anita Martínez lived on it now, in a house made of adobe with a peaked roof, and geraniums that had been planted in long, thick beds of white stone that ran along each side of the front door.

Anita was an old woman, but the first time I saw her, she came out of her house as I shut the car door, drawn up straight, reaching her arms into the air. Her black sleeves opened like wings. *"Vete de aquí!"* she yelled. "Get out!"

As I tried to explain that my great-great-grandmother had lived on her land years ago, she took a few steps towards me, and I saw the deep creases in the dark skin of her face and the startling light-blue eyes. "I was born here," she told me. "I live on this land."

When she turned and walked back into her house, the door fell shut behind her, and I got in my car and drove through fields of beans, corn, and alfalfa, past the apple and olive trees, back to the main road.

I do not remember how many times I returned to Anita's before she let me in and allowed me to ask her about

Abigail. I had found a place to stay temporarily, a nearby orchard where I could camp at night and pick fruit during the day, and I had most of my savings with me, enough to live off of for some time.

From the beginning, Anita and her granddaughter Julia watched me walk towards their house with pale, quiet eyes. They moved slowly, cautiously. Later I would learn that Anita's youngest daughter had been a professor of mathematics at a university in California. She had become pregnant and decided to raise the baby herself as a single parent. When she died in a car accident three years after Julia's birth, Julia had come to live with Anita.

It was a language of loss in which Anita spoke to me. "Owl screech all through the night, and then I knew." Or, "This is the place of ghosts. The desert brings it back." And, "Dust devils everywhere that summer. The air was black with them."

She told me about her daughter, how her black hair would fly through the wind she made, running. When her daughter was a young child, Anita used to build a wood fire in the mud oven, emptying green chiles on the red coals. "These roasted peppers I would peel, and oh, my daughter would say these are the best thing she has ever tasted."

The afternoon before Anita let me inside, I had driven out to see her but she had left me standing on her porch. The red peppers she had been threading rolled at my feet, and I thought of what they could feed in me, bright as the wing-flash of an oriole.

That next morning when I knocked again, she watched me through the screen, then opened the door, gesturing that I should step inside. The sigh that came out of her, a slight hollow sound as she closed the door, spiraled away from her house, out into the valley, over the mountains. *"Esta tierra es mía."* I saw the web of her face, how her shoulders slumped. "I lived here since my birth, and all my children were born here."

"I only want to know about Abigail Conklin," I told her again. "I could show you the letters." I had them with me, tucked inside the bag I carried.

But Anita turned her back to me, and so I followed her into the kitchen. "I've seen the court records," I told her. "I know you got the land from Abigail. Did you work for her?"

Her laughter unraveled, circling the room. When the sound finally ended, she wiped her hands across the dark skirt of her dress and then rubbed them with white cream from a shallow dish that sat on the table. "You would suck everything dry."

Later she poured thick coffee into a cup and said to the child, "This lady, so pale, like a ghost," setting it in front of me.

"No, really. I'm Abigail Reynolds," I told her again. "My great-great-grandmother lived on this land."

"Crazy. Or some *bruja*." She sat across from me, the child in her lap. "Then drink if you are no ghost." I swallowed and felt the thick coffee burn first my tongue and the roof of my mouth, then the curve of my throat.

"Ha!" The old woman nodded when I gasped. "It is hot." She brought a plate of thin cookies to the table, offered one to me, and then set the plate in front of Julia.

As the coffee pulsed through me, the room spun with heat, bright tiles around the sink the color of sky through the window, whitewashed walls shimmering. "You come again," Anita told me. And as I followed her to the door, I didn't think to ask her why I must leave or why I could return.

"I will make *sopaipillas* for you. Have you eaten them?"

Stepping out into the bright air, I shook my head. In the months to come, I would spend many hours in Anita's kitchen, drinking the coffee she kept in the blue-enameled kettle at the back of the stove and eating *sopaipillas* and *tamales* and *enchiladas*.

She would tell me about years of drought and how her grandmother Teresa buried cloth or stones the color of turquoise, then prayed that the sky would see what was under the ground, would want what it saw, a piece of itself, and storm down after it.

She would show me how to make *nixtamal*, soaking whole kernels of dried corn with lime in an enameled kettle.

Sitting in the late-autumn sun, she would tell me about riding up into the mountains each fall with her husband to gather piñons, spreading sheets on the ground and shaking the trees, roasting the nuts all winter in the fire.

The first morning I entered Anita's house, Julia's dark eyes followed me. Later I would see that the child had the ability to move like wind or water and that her laughter, like light, could go everywhere. Before I left her grandmother's house that first day, she slipped her hand into mine and let it rest there a moment, thin, warm, and dark, before pulling it away.

Her grandmother touched me also, lightly on the shoulders. "Abigail Conklin," she whispered as she shut the door after watching me drink the hot coffee. "She was my grandmother."

The

Letters

$\mathcal{C}hapter$ 1

June 15, 1867

Dearest Maggie,

I am in high spirits despite Mother's refusal to say goodbye to us. I know you are right when you said she is only fearful of "losing any more of her slender family" and wants to "gather us around her until she feels the semblance of normalcy again," but, Maggie, she must be reasonable. All of Clayton's family's property is gone. I hope you and Aunt Celia will be able to help her see the sense in what I must do.

The feather tick you gave us and all of our other belongings are tucked beneath the white linen wagon cover drawn tight to the sideboard. Some nights we sleep in our wheeled home, but if there is time, Clayton sets up the tent and we have more room to lie about.

Yesterday when we stopped for lunch, I laid out a table cloth and napkins and we ate our picnic in style. For breakfast I cook a pot of mush and milk, and brown the coffee in a frying pan. I am thankful we have our provisions, the bags of flour and the dried apples, rice, sugar, and coffee.

The land we travel through is thick with trees, and the trees are thick with heavy green leaves. After the wagons had circled this evening, I went under their cover to find some wild onions to cook with supper. I turned around in the green light once or twice, picking a few mushrooms, and could not find my way out. The light fell through a hole in the tree tops and lit the spot like an altar in a magnificent church. I thought how I could easily stay there, living off mushrooms and green light while the rest of them went westward. But, of course, I soon heard voices—the men herding the stock—and stepped out into the clearing. Since then I live in fear that Amy or Josh will wander into the trees and become a forest child, never to return to my arms again.

I watch Sally and am uneasy; I know she will wish for a doctor when her time comes. Rachel cries often, sometimes sitting in the dirt refusing to move. Sally tugs at her, begs and admonishes, "Look, Rachel, they're leaving us behind," her voice lost in the dust the mules kick up. I carry Rachel on my back often as I can, but Josh begs to be picked up also, and I cannot carry them both.

When the woods are broken by a small farm or town, we go to the doors asking to buy fresh milk or eggs or meat, but most everyone lost their animals during the war. We pass large farms where everything—homes, barns, outbuildings—has been burned, the ground slashed with black scars. I gave a whole bag of our flour to a woman with two small children and a grandmother to feed. She could not get her crops in last summer and lived off roots all winter. Her husband, Robert Collins, went to the Academy with our Davey and fought in the Fifth Cavalry.

She cried when she saw the flour. "I lost everyone," she told me, "except these children and my granny." The old woman rocked back and forth in a worn rocker on the porch, her eyes lost in a wide hole that had been their barn. "But as long as there are Christians on this earth . . ." Her tears wet my hands, which she held. She made me see again how lucky I am to have Clayton.

I must get some rest, as I am up before sunrise mixing biscuits and stirring the porridge. We sleep well in our wagon bed—the children between Clayton and me—our feathered nest.

Your Loving Sister,
Abigail

June 25, 1867
Dear Maggie,

Ten long days have passed, and I have finally stolen a few minutes by the lantern to write to you. The men insist on arriving in California no later than November, and unless we use nearly all the daylight to travel, we will get behind schedule.

Josh fell from the wagon. I don't know how it happened, except that he is always wanting to be out running in the dust. I heard his small cry smothered by the creaking of the wagon wheels as I was dressing Amy, jumped down, and thanked God out loud he was not crushed by a wheel. Roger and Sally, who were behind us, had stopped, having seen him fall. I scooped up my baby and insisted he stay put in the bed the rest of the day. Hours later, he still whimpered and cried out when he was jostled and bounced back and forth. I am certain the bone needs to be set, as he has not used the leg in two days, but Clayton insists it is only a sprain and will heal. There is no stopping.

Amy too is full of mischief. She begs to follow the older children to "collect berries" or "pick daisies by the woods," but gets lost in her own make-believe and lags behind. I am afraid she will wander right off into the wilderness! And already there is talk among us of the Indians. Everyone here is anxious about seeing them, and there is so much fear among some of the women, it is a wonder not more of us have fainted.

Last night shortly after Clayton and I had lain down, the Captain yelled out, "Indians!" and the entire train was thrown into confusion. The men grabbed their guns, and more than a few of them ran into one another while attempting to rush to their posts. A number of women screamed, and most were too frightened to get out of their bedding. I crouched beside our wagon gripping a loaded rifle, which Clayton had taught me to use. Fortunately, it did not discharge itself. We will need more drills before reaching Indian territory.

Hettie Shallot claims the Indians are all savages and after murdering our husbands will strap us to their horses, carry us back to their tribe, and force us to be their wives. She has elaborate plans for extinguishing herself if—I should say when—she hears their yelps and looks up from her sleep to see a painted face staring down at her and a tomahawk swinging above her.

Bea finds all this talk of "savages" amusing and says the Indians "will surely leave Hettie alone if they hear her fierce tongue." Sally turns away from the campfire when any talk of Indians starts up, and climbs into her wagon, pulling the flaps closed for the night. If the baby is born in Indian territory, the wagon train won't be able to stop, and being a lone wagon somewhere in the middle of the Indian frontier is unthinkable.

Your Loving Sister,

Abigail

July 1, 1867

Dearest Maggie,

Josh still limps when he tries to walk, but he has stopped crying out and so I am hopeful of his recovery. Our journey proceeds slowly but steadily; each day we are closer to the Mississippi. We have crossed two rivers, and both being low, we were able to ford the wagons across. The Conners' milk cow got poisoned by eating jimsonweed and is sorely missed, as it provided many of us with some milk.

Bea Manning and I are becoming fast friends. I know Mother disapproves of her because she is "too outspoken" and more independent "than a lady should be," but she also has a good deal of common sense and a delightful sense of humor. The "gymnasium costume" she wears, the short wool skirt with full bloomer pants fastening at the knee, is more practical than any of my calico dresses. Yesterday when Hettie complained loudly over having to travel on Sunday, which of course we must do to stay on schedule, Bea turned to me with her hands pressed together in prayer, thanking God in earnest that she would not have to sit through one of Father Davis's sermons, and declared walking itself a kind of worship.

I pulled her to the side of the trail and, when the others had passed us, told her about the paints and canvases I hid in the bottom of the wagon. "Clayton would promptly dump them out if he knew," I said. "Unnecessary weight. Besides, he doesn't want me spending my time painting when there's baking and sewing and gardening to be done."

"I brought my favorite books folded up in a towel and stuffed in my pillow case," she told me. "I've also got my best ink pens under the silverware. They can't expect us to leave everything that is civilized behind."

What will I do for company once we reach New Mexico? If you and your family did not plan to follow us soon, I would indeed have difficulty leaving the others to go on to California without us. Clayton thinks only of reaching New Mexico in time to investigate the mining opportunities he has been offered. I have implored him to consider staying with the others and settling in California, as you suggested, near San Francisco or San Diego, where Bea says there are schools and churches and roads with shops, but he does not hear me. He claims that land is the same everywhere and that we can farm it in New Mexico as well as we could in California. With the money he insists he will earn mining in

New Mexico, he is sure that before long we will be ahead there. But to be without churches and schools, without all these civilizing forces that make a community!

Oh, to be in your arms again, Sister, and hear your soothing advice!

Abigail

July 8, 1867

Dearest Maggie,

Today we crossed the Mississippi, and what a grand river it is, with rich fertile land far as you can see on either side and lovely willows arching towards the water from the bank. We were ferried across and had to take the wagon wheels off and carry everything onto rafts, piling them high with our goods. The rafts were pulled to the other side by a pulley that stretched across the water. The whole operation took most of the day, as we were pulled downstream by the current and had to be towed to the landing before the load could be taken off.

Josh and Amy were lit with the excitement of it. I had to grasp each one firmly by the hand, or they would have been off into the deep, cool water and down the wide Mississippi heading for New Orleans, but we had no casualties and did not lose any of the stock, which they took across by tying the ropes to the horns of the oxen and around the necks of the mules and horses. This westward crossing is not as dangerous as we feared!

I know Mother could not possibly comprehend how we women accomplish the daily chores of life here on the trail, but I hope, Sister, that you will try. Not only do we do our own cooking, but we must manage it without a stove. To-night I baked a skillet of corn bread over hot rocks to have as a treat from our regular fare of beans and coffee. Some afternoons I work dough in my hands as I walk. In the evenings we women cook beans over the open fire; sometimes a little biscuit is made to go with them. Clean-up consists of finding a stream. You would not believe the expense of everyday staples we take for granted in Virginia. Milk costs twenty-five cents for a quart bottle, so we only give it to the children. Eggs and chickens are just as expensive.

Last night shortly before dawn, we heard a weak war whoop, followed by the cry of "Indians!" We soon learned it was a false alarm given by Mr. Tanner, who delights in all kinds of practical jokes, such as roping together the legs of a friend's oxen. A number of shotguns were lifted and two were fired. There was a woman who fainted. When the excitement was ended, several of the men went off into the woods led by Mr. Tanner, convinced, I think, that if they searched hard enough a real Indian might turn up.

The rest of us readied the wagons for an early start, and I am sure Clayton and I were not the only ones who had visions of stringing up our humorous companion for depriving us of even a little of our much-needed sleep. Tomorrow is Sunday, and we will have a day of rest before we head out across Arkansas, but I will need to spend it washing dust from our clothing with the water we've saved in rain barrels. All of our clothes will require plenty of scrubbing.

As we get closer to the frontier, Clayton claims he is tired of the wooded countryside and boasts he will welcome the wide, open frontier of the southwest, but I fear I will miss the gentle dogwoods and the shade the oak trees give us from the heat. I cannot imagine a land empty of them.

Your Sister,
Abigail

July 16, 1867

My Dearest Sister,

We are now crossing Arkansas. The trail is rockier and the woods are a dense mass of greens and browns. Very little of the land here has been cultivated, and the trees and brush seem to grow whichever tangled way they want. I look into the distance and watch a hawk, wings spread wide, dip and sway across the trees and know this is a place that has not been tamed. Each night there is talk around the campfire of wildcats and bears as we stare out into the thick trees and listen for the snapping of twigs and branches.

During the days it has been so hot that Josh and Amy cry most of the time. Bedding them down to ride in the wagon just makes them hotter, as there is not enough air and the sun turns the wagon into an oven. When I dip rags in water and wipe the dust off them, Clayton tells me not to waste the water. I know he is right, but it's just a little I put on the rag. We are all tanned and sunburned, even the ladies, despite the bonnets we wear. Amy has pulled the doll you made into shreds, carrying it with her all day as she walks, refusing to leave it in the wagon. I intend to sew the pieces together once we are stopped long enough for me to dig out my needles and thread.

Yesterday evening when the wagons had circled, Roger came for me. I climbed into his wagon, everything going dark the way it does after you have walked under the bright, bright sky all day, so that I had to follow the lines of the wagon—the cloth sides, the wooden box packed with dishes and clothing, the blankets folded across the bed—to find Sally's curled shape. She was holding the cloth pillow cover I had watched her embroider sitting on Mama's porch shortly after her marriage.

I sat down on the wagon bed. Her face was hot as a

coal from the campfire. She opened her eyes, narrow slits of whiteness, saw that I was there, and closed them again. "Go get more help," I said to Roger, who stood at the end of the wagon, his mouth wide open with me ordering him.

The blood had soaked through the quilt Sally's mama had sewn. "The baby's not moving," she whispered as I tried to prop her up against the side of the wagon. "I was afraid to tell Roger. They can't stop the whole train for one woman having a baby."

It was after midnight before the baby was born. If Anna's mother had not been there, we would have lost Sally, that baby turned wrong and it taking every bit of strength Mrs. Vernon had to pull it out right. Even with Mrs. Vernon there, I thought for a good while we would lose Sally, her life running out, soaking the mattress. I kept remembering when we were girls, the three of us climbing that oak tree beside her house, the sound our dresses made, ripping.

"Heart-friends cannot be parted," she said to me once. Next to you, whom I miss more than I can write, she is my oldest and dearest friend. The thought of losing her on the trail before we reached New Mexico was one I could not bear.

The baby is a boy, with a head full of hair dark as Sally's. He has not cried above a whimper. Sally cannot stand yet. I stayed in the wagon with her most of the morning. She winced each time the wagon bumped or jolted, and bit her lip to keep from crying out. Bea says our lot is harder than a man's, because war or no war, we have to face child-birth. I suppose she is right.

Your Loving Sister,
Abigail

July 18, 1867

Dear Maggie,

Sally's baby boy died this morning. We buried it beside the trail but left no marker, so that the Indians would not find it. They say the Indians dig up the dead for their cloth-ing and jewelry, sometimes taking their scalps. Sally was too weak to leave the wagon, so I helped Roger place the poor little thing in a rough box he had fashioned the night before when he saw it was dying.

Sally wanted the baby dressed in the christening gown and cap she had brought from home. When I carried the baby to her before we laid it in the box, I started to set him in her lap, but she reached up and touched the fine lace on the christening gown, smoothing it between her fingers. Fi-nally, she dropped her hand and turned her head towards the sky, which showed a deep blue already through the opening of the wagon. "I would give anything for a picture of him that I could keep," she said to that brightness.

I handed the baby to Roger, who was standing beside the wagon. He set the baby in the box, but before we buried it, I took out the paper I had slipped under our bedding and my pencils and made a quick sketch of him. If there is time later, I will fill in the features with a little color. Last night I showed the drawing to Sally, and while it made her cry, I feel certain she will be glad to have it.

We have seen our first Indians this past week. Sometimes they follow us for miles, and when we stop to eat they beg for food. There was a young woman among them who wept for nearly an hour, until Bea and I felt sorry for her and gave her a jar of jelly.

Some of the Indians are nearly naked, while others are dressed in any imaginable combination of attire. The Indian braves often wear trousers, but it is not uncommon to see a squaw in a pair of them held up around her waist with a rope of buckhide. Indeed, I have also seen Indian maidens dressed in nothing but necklaces of turquoise and silver and brass. The children of both sexes tend to go completely naked, and just when we have begun to pity the poverty of the whole lot, one of the men rides by fully clothed and decorated with a profusion of silver.

Yesterday afternoon when Sally and I stopped to rest for a few moments beneath a tree, we were startled by the approach of a rather handsome Indian wearing a finely made linen shirt with a long-tailed jacket and absolutely nothing else except a pair of moccasins. He offered us a deerskin, but we were too overcome by his appearance to consider what we could trade him for it. Later I overheard that someone in our party gave him some counterfeit greenbacks for it. Had I been present, I would have warned the fashionable, if partially clad, savage of the deceit.

The Indians are not, however, always on the receiving side of the trickery. More than once we have gone in search of non-existent streams after being "educated" as to their whereabouts by a "helpful" Indian or squaw. They have scattered our stock, then made off with some of our supplies while the majority of our party was involved with rounding up cows, oxen, and horses. Most of their pranks are simply a nuisance, but I fear the open land to come, which is roamed by Comanches, one of the most unfriendly tribes of the prairie. These warriors are anxious to attack white settlers and string up large numbers of scalps. We have had more Indian drills, most of which the Captain has judged successful. I suppose we are prepared to meet them.

I have several letters now that need posting and will bundle them together to send once we reach Fort Smith. It is like having you next to me, Sister, each time I write. I can almost hear your soft, reassuring voice in the emptiness next to me at the fireside.

Oh! How I wish I had you in my arms!

Abigail

July 27, 1867

Dear Maggie,

When we reached Fort Smith, your letters were waiting (all five of them, and they were glorious!), with one from Aunt Celia, but nothing from Mother. I have written to her again this morning, encouraging her to do as you suggest, sell off the farm for what she can and move into Aunt Celia's home. I don't see how she can pay the taxes this year, not when they have gone up and she has no crop to bring in.

I doubt Mother will hear me on this or any issue, but I pray that she will listen to your good advice, and please, Maggie, if you are able, explain to her again that with so many of the businesses shut down and the land Clayton's family had owned bought out from under them by Yankees, he was unable to earn a living. We have no wish to live in poverty, dependent on the good will of others, and must go where our futures best lie. It is, of course, your decision to

delay telling her of your own plans to follow us. I believe
in being forthright on all occasions, but perhaps you are right
to wait; it has been difficult enough for her to accept our
leaving. I am sure her state of mind will improve as your
time draws near. Oh, that I were there for that blessed event!

At the fort we saw plenty of soldiers. They are well
armed and barricaded against any attacks. Another wagon
train passed through while we were stopped, and we saw
several stage and mail coaches. Westward immigration is vast.
We were told of hundreds who pass through there.

Each day the land becomes flatter and more barren of
trees. But there is still plenty of grass for the stock, and the
roads are easily traveled. If I were able to paint this land, I
would use a yellow-green wash and have it meet the blue of
the horizon in one straight line. A deep brown patched with
white would do for the rocks and boulders scattered along
the roadside, and our train would be a thin winding line of
grays, browns, and bits of blue, red, yellow, and pink. A
small dark streak would dip towards the horizon like the
hawks that follow our small train across the plains.

I spend much of each day walking beside the wagon or
the oxen, carrying Josh. It is a relief when I am able to ride
on the wagon seat and roll our dough for supper. Sometimes
we sight Indians in the woods or watch them following our
train at a distance. They like to trade and usually come out
ahead in the bargain. Fred Tapens traded his watch for a

horse, which we later learned had been stolen from the train just ahead of us. Of course, he was obliged to give back the stolen goods and is now minus his watch. A few days ago a tall, rather good-looking brave offered Clayton two ponies as a trade for me. The ponies were a sandy-brown color, strong and healthy looking. Perhaps it would have been a good bargain.

Just outside Fort Smith we met up with another, larger wagon train, and what a break in the monotony was had by all! We spent much of the night dancing to the music of a fiddler. If Indians crouched in the darkness watching as they sometimes do, I don't know what they thought of us and our strange, pale-faced whooping and dancing. Clayton and I twirled across the wide grassy plains. Roger coaxed Sally out of the wagon, and her cheeks flushed as she watched us.

The sky here spreads over and over the land—there is more of it than you could imagine. When Clayton and I walked back to the wagon it wrapped around us, the milky stars woven against the dark.

"It's as if the universe were holding us cupped in the center of its hand," I said to Clayton.

When he did not say anything back, I stopped walking, letting the dark and light get between us, afraid he was thinking of some harm that had come to Josh and Amy, who were asleep in the tent. But he stopped and turned, looked straight at me before saying what was in his mind. "I was thinking about tomorrow and the next day," he said. "Thinking about the rest of the crossing."

I reached across the vastness to squeeze his hand. "We did right, coming."

He looked away from me, out into the sky. The wind picked up, and the sky was everywhere. I felt it sift through my hair and thought how with each breath its light and dark filled me. "I just hope you say that five years from now. The trip out here is hard enough, and New Mexico won't be easy either. Mostly Indians and Mexicans."

"We could keep going with the others." It was what I had been saying over and over in my heart ever since we left Virginia. "There is mining in California also, plenty of it."

He looked towards the wagon. "The mines I know about are in New Mexico. That's where Mr. Stone is, and he knows me, knows my work. I told him I would manage his mines there." We were walking towards the campsite again. Even in the darkness I could see the wagon's billowing shape, the thin spokes of each wheel which seem, even when the wagon is still, to spin endlessly. "I'll get a chance to buy in, too." Clayton kept talking. "I could make some real money there, and think, Abigail, of the land we could buy with it, our own land."

When we crawled into the tent, the air, still warm from the day's heat, was filled with the soft breathing of the children. We lay down on either side of Amy and Josh, and I tried not to feel bitter. There are plenty of jobs in California and plenty of mines. First to leave you and Mama and Aunt Celia, in another two or three months to say goodbye to Sally and Bea and the rest of them!

But when Amy's small warmth snuggled against me, I told myself that once we reached New Mexico I would still have what is most important right beside me. Only I wish Virginia were not so far away!

Your Loving Sister,
Abigail

August 18, 1867

My Dear Maggie,

Last week I saw my first Comanche brave. I had heard quite a few stories of the "red devils who attack entire wagon trains, whooping and screaming, swinging tomahawks and shooting off rifles." This "brave" stood proudly with his arms crossed, several yards from the road, watching us pass, wearing nothing but a discarded hoop from a woman's skirt. Sally, Bea, and I laughed until we could hardly walk. He stuck his chin out farther and proudly looked down his nose at us. Sometime later when we looked back across the flat plain we saw his sharp unmoving profile.

Many of those in our party rant against the Indians, calling them beggars and thieves and murderers. We heard of a white woman's body found near here on the bank of a creek, a piece of hair rope around her neck. Men from another wagon train burned a small Indian encampment. When the Indians returned and discovered which group was to blame, they attacked, stealing some of the stock. A child was killed by the stampeding horses.

Still, I would like to paint the Indians. Some of the women wear gowns beaded with small stones and shells in patterns. Their skin is a deep rust color, their hair dark and thick. Yesterday evening an Indian danced for me after I gave him a cooking pot. One moment he was an antelope, the next a bird winging across the vast horizon; then he mirrored the mountains themselves. He danced his last steps and vanished as if by magic. The children, Bea, and I watched without moving, we were so astonished. After the Indian had disappeared, I learned to my horror that Clayton had gone to the wagon to retrieve his shotgun.

Now that we are on the plains, we occasionally see other wagon camps. Tales float back and forth of bands of Indians or bushwhackers or renegades. There are said to be plenty of white renegades who have taken up with the Indians, and others ride in packs, thieving and killing. A good number of them are said to paint their skin and dress like Indians. They are called "white Indians," and one can often recognize them because they get lazy with their painting and leave their legs white.

Despite the tales that circulate the wagon trains, most of what we see is interesting and quite harmless. We pass forts or trading posts where we can get water and needed supplies. A few of the forts have been abandoned, and we walk through their crumbling adobe walls. We pass Mexicans with their burros, and a few days ago we saw Mexican cattle drivers.

The road grows hotter each day as we pass through Texas. Josh and Amy cry from the heat. I sing to them as we walk, and make up stories. "This is where a buffalo was shot by Indians," I tell them, and Amy traces the imprint in the dirt with her hand. "This is where two Indian girls played with the dolls their mothers made them," Amy says. Josh still fusses, and I end up carrying him much of the way.

We have filled our kegs and everything that will hold water, which we must divide with the oxen. Whenever we stop, we carry them a bucket and let them wet their tongues and wash the dust off their noses. Occasionally a stage coach passes us, and I think they must look with pity on our plodding pace.

Sally is able to walk again. She worries about losing Rachel to Indians or sickness before they reach California. Yesterday we passed a fenced-in grave site, the markers for two brothers, dead within a day of each other from cholera.

We have passed a number of such graves, and sometimes there are several of them standing together. It took both Martha and me to pull Sally away, and she would not let go of Rachel's hand the rest of the afternoon, carrying the child on her back when she complained, much as I begged her to put Rachel in the wagon and save her strength.

Your Sister,
Abigail

September 3, 1867

Dear Maggie,

Last night we heard of more Indian killings. A band of Indians attacked a wagon train some ten miles ahead of ours, killing six of the men and one woman and her child. They plundered one of the wagons, stealing all that was in it, including several hundred dollars, the bags of grain, and the yoke of oxen, then they shot the little girl who lay inside the wagon four times.

This morning the Captain decided we would proceed anyway, armed and ready against all attacks, but Sally refused to go on, saying she would burn the wagon if Roger did not agree to turn back east. I know you cannot imagine our meek

Sally threatening thus, but Maggie, this land is nothing like Virginia, and every one of us has been changed by it.

Roger does not have much patience. He attempted to pick her up bodily and throw her into the wagon, and when she kicked and screamed that she would walk back carrying Rachel, he cuffed her. Clayton said that any woman gone crazy needed the sense knocked into her and warned me not to interfere, but I ran towards them, pulled at Roger's arm until he stopped long enough to hear me.

"Sally's not in her right mind," I told him. All that she lost—her child, her brother, and her first husband—were in my head.

When Roger let go of her, I told him to hitch up his wagon, that I would see that she came.

"I'm not leaving her to get her own way back," he said in his defense, and then went on about the dangers of traveling back alone and how their only safety was to stay with the wagon train, until finally I saw how scared he was, and I pitied him.

The land is dry, with little vegetation. At first I thought it had no color, as everything except the sky seemed gray or brown. But these last few days I look out across the land and see that the brown is mixed with different shades of red and even orange. And there are plants. One that grows in abundance is given the name "prairie torch." It has stiff sharp leaves and a tall flower stalk that shoots up into the air and is covered with small yellow blossoms. Yesterday we traveled through a field of what Sally is sure were bluebonnets. I would give anything to see the field in the spring when thousands of deep-blue blossoms cover both sides of the trail.

The day before yesterday there was a windstorm, and we had to make camp early. The road was nearly all sand, and some of the wagons had sunk to their hubs. The oxen strained under pulling their load. We were stopped for a day and a half, and the children enjoyed this inconvenience as if it were a holiday, "visiting" with their friends in the other wagons or curling up with a favorite plaything under a comforter, protected from the wind by the wagon's canvas.

When the storm died, Mr. Garfield rode out to hunt buffalo and returned with his feet swollen up from the needles of the prickly pears. Needless to say, there was no buffalo hide. The men do hunt antelope, deer, and fox. Every so often we pass a ranch with a well of good water and are able to stop and refresh ourselves. Some days I feel sick from all the heat and exhaustion, but we keep moving.

We have seen mud houses, which we are told are the huts of Mexicans or Indians. The few Indians that came to our camp tonight were peaceful, but as you can imagine, we were wary. They seemed to know nothing of the killings and were impressed with my blond-headed child, stroking his hair and commenting to one another about it. A young Indian woman who was with them was pock-marked. They have contracted small pox from us and do not know what it is that kills them. It is said that they get it from digging up our dead for the clothes and jewelry.

Please tell Mother that we will reach New Mexico in a few weeks. If the land is as inexpensive and as rich as we hear, perhaps she will come out with you and John when you join us! I am so anxious to see all of you,

My loved ones,
Abigail

September 27, 1867

Dearest Maggie,

Oh, how can I tell you? Maggie, I do not know if I can write this down on paper and send it to you. My baby is gone, drowned by the Pecos River. Two days ago now, and still all last night I spent searching for him. Clayton woke me as I was sifting through the bed clothes before light. "Stop," he said. "Lie still and sleep." But how can I when Josh, my littlest, is gone?

"You made me leave him," I cry out, even when I do sleep. I wanted to make a bed for him in the wagon, carry him with us to New Mexico. But Clayton insisted on burying him beside the trail, not even a picket fence to keep the wolves away. Five hours I carried him limp and bluish in my arms, still Josh with his glistening white hair, I carried him until every strand was dry and pulled the gown I'd sewn for him last winter over his head and carried him some more, and he was sweet-smelling and soft. "Please let me bring him," I begged Clayton. "It is only two weeks more, maybe three." To leave him when we were so close.

It was near dark, and Clayton had the shovel. The sound of him breaking hard clay. "Go to Amy," he kept telling me. "Leave his body alone now. Go to her." He thinks my mind is gone. His voice is soft, but his eyes are hard on me as the dirt he breaks.

Abigail

October 1, 1867

Dearest Maggie,

I will put this down now and say it all. Do not tell Mama and Aunt Celia, not yet. We had paid the Indians to ferry us across the Pecos River at Horsehead Crossing. There was no other way, as the river was wide and too deep for oxen or wagons. I had the children in the front of the wagon. The current was swift, we knew this, but it was a calm, still day, heat and light shimmering off the water. I sat with the children before crossing and watched the dragon flies light on the water with their clear, transparent wings.

The crossing seemed easy; the Indians and their strong rafts a blessing. Roger and Sally were behind us, and I leaned out of our wagon and waved to them. Then, part way across, as water lapped against the raft and Amy and Josh peered out from inside the wagon, I heard someone yelling before the shots were fired. Carl Thomas had discovered a small chest missing. He accused the Indians of stealing it, shooting at them, and us dependent on them for our lives. Carl's raft overturned, and I felt ours sway, the wagon almost rolling off, going under. I had Amy's hand, but when I reached for Josh there was nothing. Clayton dove for him, but when he brought the child up, there was nothing even the old Indian, who tried a good part of the morning, could do.

Sister, I have cut some of his hair to keep but do not have even a picture of him to carry.

Your Sister,
Abigail

$\mathcal{C}$hapter 2

November 12, 1867

Dear Maggie,

We have settled in one of the mining towns in the southwest part of the New Mexico territory. Mr. Carlton and the Prestons and Mr. Howell decided to stop here also. There is gold fever in this area, and hundreds of people have come to these newly risen towns to make their fortunes. Clayton is investigating a vein, which they are digging out of the bedrock. Meanwhile, we are living in a tent camp with at least a hundred other miners and their families. Some of the shelters are made of carpets or bedding hung on ropes. Fortunately, our tent serves us well. We have dug it into a hillside for added warmth and spread the wagon cover on the ground as a floor.

One sees every kind of person here: Chinamen wearing their strange, colorful jackets and small black caps, Mexicans, hearty, rugged men who have come down from the mountains of Colorado, and those, like us, come from the east. The camp is populated mostly with men, but there are a few families. Our immediate neighbors are the Prestons, who have three boys, the youngest of whom is eight. I spend afternoons with Mrs. Preston, or Mira as she insists I call her, planning and cooking an evening meal. This is no easy feat, as there is no fresh food to be had here and we are forced to live off our staples of flour, sugar, meal, and dried apples. Clayton and Mr. Carlton have been successful at hunting the deer and antelope, so we occasionally add meat to our meals of biscuits and cooked grain. I have had to cook out-of-doors over a fire, heating the food on a pile of red-hot rocks, and we eat out of cups and plates of tin.

There are many rough men to be found in the camp. A good portion of them are disappointed to learn the gold must be dug out of the ground. I think they envisioned themselves scooping it up with their hands, as if something that precious would have been scattered across the desert by fairies. Their disappointment often turns to anger, and Maggie, this is a corrupt place full of gambling and fighting.

There was a man killed two nights ago in the camp, shot dead, and there was talk of riding down the ones that did it and hanging them.

Each day nearly bursts with the pitch of excitement, someone screaming, "Gold, Gold!" or the blast of a gun. I could hardly stand it except that the mountains nearby cut such an amazingly clear and vibrant line against the wide, seamless sky. I never tire of looking at it.

How are you and John and the children? Amy still asks for her cousin Irene. We do miss all of you.

Your Sister,

Abigail

December 12, 1867

Dear Maggie,

I was ecstatic to get your news. I am sure Alexander is a beauty, and I know how glad you are to have Mother nearby. We have moved to another camp, near the river. Clayton is helping to establish a mill, and we have secured a "house" for the winter. It is really no more than a one-room shelter built of rough pine boards, but we have a small stove to heat it with. While Clayton is away, making his fortune, Amy and I spend our days in the camp, where I am paid to cook for several of the men.

There is another woman, living in a shelter next to ours, a Mrs. Norris, but she is afraid of her husband, who is cross and sullen and likely at any time of day to come home, so I do not visit often with her. She came over yesterday to sit by the stove and have a cup of tea, and I wanted to find some words that would ease her. She is less than twenty years and married without more than a month's engagement. Marriage can be a blessing or a curse, and I suppose none of us guesses to what extent we have sealed our fates when we agree to pledge ourselves with a ring.

There is an actual town here, with a dry goods store, but the prices are so steep I was unable to purchase anything. The currency is in gold dust or nuggets, which are carried in small bottles and weighed on scales. They look like glass filled with sky glitter, a child's play pretty.

While we were encamped by the first mine, Clayton traded our oxen for a pair of horses, so they are now our means of travel. Some afternoons, if it is warm enough, Amy and I ride out in the wagon along a creek bed or to see the mines and the mill where they grind the ores that are dug from the ground. I still cannot get used to the sky, how blue in color it is and how much of it there is, sky, sky, sky stretching over this piece of desert. Clayton says I am "sky-crazy," and I suppose he is right. It seems, to me, full of promise.

Your Sister,
Abigail

January 14, 1868

Dear Maggie,

We have lasted more than a month now in our wooden shack. I spend much of each day preparing breakfast and dinner for the men, but they are kind to me and appreciate any small treat I am able to give them, a few potatoes mixed in with the soup, well-risen bread.

I have done some work for Mrs. Wilson of Kansas, helping with her three children as she has a new baby. I do the sewing and cooking, whatever I have time for. They live in a more permanent structure, with a wood floor, and it is pleasant for Amy to sit playing by their stove in the afternoons while I do a few of the chores. She pays me in gold dust, and so I have accumulated nearly as much as Clayton. Her husband has found so much of it that they nearly sprinkle it around the house.

Mrs. Wilson is pleasant and a gossip, so I have learned

the comings and goings of the town. There were three men killed last week in a saloon fight. Mr. Norris is suspected of having been involved. His wife had confided to me earlier that day her hopes of escaping him. She had planned to ride with another couple to Colorado, where she hoped to look for her family. But the story is that Mr. Norris returned in the night and took her with him. No one knows where they have gone, what stretch of desert or cliff or mountain.

There are numerous places where outlaws can hide. They disappear for years or turn up living in Mexico off their stolen goods. Poor Mollie, for she is a sweet girl, kind and frightened and innocent, will be dragged through the desert, and I doubt I will hear of her again unless it is her body that is found.

Mrs. Wilson claims the Norrises' shanty was searched for evidence, but none was found. Last night Clayton said that this place is too rough, with killings every week, and he stayed awake until morning, listening for bandits.

At least on the trail we were assured our company was honest and good. The Prestons have gone on to Pikes Peak, and Mr. Howell departed for California. Mr. Carlton is in a neighboring mining town. This has become a place of strangers. As soon as spring is here, we will look for a house to rent outside the mining towns.

Two days ago there was talk of an Indian raid on the mine, and they decided in the event of an attack they would lower the women and children down into the mines. I told Clayton I would prefer scalping to being buried alive, but he refused to smile and claimed I make light too much of danger. I am not as afraid of Indians as I am of some of the miners who would be lowering us in the buckets.

Oh, I will try not to be forlorn. Clayton insists that soon he will make his fortune. Any day now I shall find myself living in a mansion!

Your Sister,
Abigail

July 29, 1868

Dear Maggie,

We are settled in a small town some fifty miles from the mining towns, in what is known here as a house. It is all made of mud and a few rough timbers, with a flat roof, and the floors are earth also. We have two small rooms and a third I made by hanging a quilt. Our yard is large enough to keep a few chickens. The land is very dry and so full of sand that a windstorm can make it drift over the trees. There is a place not far from here where the sand is six inches deep, and at times one can see great drifts of it.

I have stretched scraps of bright cloth across the narrow

openings that are our only windows, and I set up the table we brought from home and the two chairs. Our bedding is rolled out on a few loose boards set directly on the ground. Amy sleeps on a bed roll in the corner of our bedroom. Small and rough as the adobe is, it seems royal after the months we spent in the tent and the dugout. The worst of it is the snakes, which come inside whenever they please. Twice I have woke in the morning, only to stare at one curled in the corner of the room. If we cannot chase them out, Clayton shoots them.

The town is quite small, with just a post office and a store that sells flour, soap, and sugar. Everywhere we hear the strange babel of tongues; there are so many foreigners here. The river is not far from us, and Clayton says we can get the water we'll need to farm the land. In front of our yard, there is sage brush and cacti, a long-thorned prickly pear and cholla, which reach for the sky with thin arms covered with a fine, sharp fuzz. Clayton jokes that he will go out and trim them the way you would trim fruit trees planted near a front porch in Virginia.

Clayton is gone at the mines three and four days at a time, so it is just me and Amy here. The quiet is a relief to me after the constant noise of the camps. I worry about Clayton crossing the desert alone, as there are plenty of Indians and Mexicans who will shoot a man for his horse, but I prefer being settled in a home far from the shoot-outs and fights. The week before we left, there were killings in the streets over gold nuggets. Clayton says that the mine had given out. He is at work on a new one now, which Mr. Stone has asked him to excavate. There is a lack of water in this region, which makes it difficult to separate the ore, but he is confident he will find a large vein.

Here, in our house of dirt, there is no one to bother us, there is no one at all to even talk with. Amy and I spend the day baking bread or sewing the clothes that got worn out on the trip. Already, she is good with a needle and thread. There is much to practice on.

It has been months since I have had a word from you. Give me news of everything. And please, now that we are settled, tell John he must set a date for when you will come and join us!

Your Loving Sister,
Abigail

November 20, 1868

Dearest Maggie,

It was a pleasure to read your letter, so full of the descriptions of your children and their small antics. I appreciate your offer to send a Christmas package. This year's holiday will not be any more bountiful than last year's. Please send some pecans, if you can, and persimmons. Amy is asking for pears. Any fruit would be most welcome. We have plenty of flour for salt-rising bread, a few dried apples, and a little coffee. I was able to purchase squash and dried corn.

Last week, when the weather turned quite cold, we woke to find frost on the bed covers and snowflakes on the table near the door. But today it is so warm I let the fire go out in the stove.

You said nothing in your letter about joining us, and I pray you are still considering making the trip. If you leave early enough in the spring, you can avoid some of the heat in Texas. It will have been two years by then since we have seen one another, too long for sisters like us to be apart. I cannot bear it.

Lovingly,
Abigail

February 2, 1869

Dear Maggie,

We were most grateful for the nuts and fruits, for the thread, lace, and notions you sent to us. There is such a lack here of everything but the basic necessities. You said nothing in your letter about joining us this spring, and instead you encouraged me to bring Amy and "come home" for a visit. I do not understand why you are so reluctant to discuss taking the trip here. I can only imagine that Mother has convinced you not to come or that John has found new business interests.

The land here is like no other in the country—the mountains are golden and the ground will be fertile when there is water. Winter is so mild we have used very little fuel. Clayton says to tell John that there are mines full of gold, silver, and copper. Clayton has bought a share in two of them and will purchase a share for you before you come if you send him the money. There is much opportunity to prosper. Several ranches south of here stretch for miles and include horses and sheep and fields planted in cotton, corn, and all kinds of fruits and vegetables. Some of the best families from Virginia and Georgia and Tennessee live in Mesilla. Clayton has promised me a trip there this summer.

Yesterday I hauled some sawdust, which we use to put up our own ice, and spent the rest of the afternoon scrubbing our clothing. Clayton needs new trousers but will get by for the present with the ones I have put a new seat on. Mending seems an endless chore. I have put new fronts on my aprons, hoping they will hide the wear my skirts have taken.

Last fall I traded some gold dust for a bag of turnips, which were such a treat that we ate them only a few at a time. They disappeared last month; then yesterday I found them, frozen hard in a nest some rats had made, nestled between a candle and a missing handkerchief of mine. The rats had made themselves quite comfortable, living off our "luxuries."

I do hope all is well with you and the little ones. This spring we will plant the seeds for our first set of crops. And I hope we will see you here before summer.

Your Devoted Sister,
Abigail

April 21, 1869

Dearest Maggie,

Please write soon and say that you are planning your trip westward to join us in building a home in the desert. I stop at least once every day and wish you here with me. I hope it will not be long before we hold one another again.

Amy has learned to amuse herself playing with the horned toads and rabbits that she finds. Since we left the mining town, she seldom has another child to play with. I worry that she misses her brother, but she does not speak of him. We have a few hens and a whole brood of chicks, which she delights in feeding. We are planting corn and all sorts of vegetables. If you can, send me some snips of black-berries and grapes, and I will try them here. We have heard talk that there is not enough water to grow crops, but with the river near by and the long growing season, we are sure of success.

Clayton will be gone to the mines much of next week, where he has invested in a number of stakes. I do not know what I would do without Amy, for she helps me with the laundry, the cleaning, and the planting. This month I have spent at least two hours every morning cleaning the dust from our bedding and the pots and pans. It seems the wind will never stop blowing.

We have few visitors. Amy loves to sit by the road and watch the Mexicans who sometimes go by with their burros, and there was a Mexican woman who came to the door yesterday with some milk to sell. I am not much afraid, even on the nights when Clayton is away, but I keep a shotgun loaded and near the bed. All kinds of outlaws roam the desert, renegades, both white and Mexican.

There is little law here, and I don't believe many of the criminals ever get to court. If they are caught they might go straight to the end of the rope, but most of them head south into Mexico and are never apprehended.

I have letters from both Bea and Sally. They have settled in a valley near San Diego. The land is rich for farming, and there is a church and a school nearby. I envy them their companionship. If Clayton had been willing, we could have stayed with the wagon train and settled with them. But perhaps he is right in saying that the land here is just as fertile and the mining opportunities are abundant.

The longer we are here, the more variety I notice in the plant life: white and purple thistles, wild sunflowers, Spanish broom. Late in the day, when part of the earth is under shade, the sage brush turns deep blue-green without the sun to bleach it gray. I believe Clayton wants to stay in this remote place because he likes striking out on his own. Yesterday he told me that he will make his fortune in mining and build us a sprawling ranch house. He plans to turn our land into the most fertile farm in the territory!

Your Sister,
Abigail

July 8, 1869

Dearest Maggie,

What news! If you are able to come join us next spring, perhaps Clayton will have expanded the house and you can

stay with us as long as you like. I have made a rocking chair
out of a barrel which I covered and a bedstead of white pine
boards. The mines are doing well, but the spring rains were
really quite sparse and summer is a dry, hot season here. We
get our water from a pump in the yard, but Clayton says
there is not enough to try to water the crops. On hot evenings, when Amy cries from the heat, I let her run out to
the pump and splash water on herself. Some evenings she
plays like that for nearly an hour. Clayton got a small goat
from a Mexican in town, and we tied it in the shade near
the house. It has become Amy's pet, and she carries it water
and a little feed. It is too small for her to ride, but she
does try!

I was much relieved to get the news that Mother has
sold the land and moved in with Aunt Celia. I don't agree
with you that father's grief over seeing our land in the possession of Yankees would have killed him if a bullet had not.
Father fought in the war nearly to its end and saw the changes
that were sure to follow. "Survival," he told me before he
left for Richmond that last time. "That is what matters most,
when the rest is stripped away." He would accept the necessary sale of the land better than Mother has. If he had
returned from the war a young man, as Clayton did, I feel
certain he too would have journeyed west.

It will be wonderful to greet you next spring. Tell John,
if he can, to send us the money soon, and Clayton will

get him a share in one of the mines. We will make our fortunes together!

Your Loving Sister,
Abigail

October 14, 1869

Dear Maggie,

I dread to tell you all that has happened. Clayton has lost the money he invested in the mines—all of our savings and the two hundred John sent not more than one month ago. The mines Clayton bought stakes in did not have enough gold in them to return the investment. He says he is finished with those mines and will move on to another, but he hasn't the money to buy any more stakes.

To make things worse, we have seen the largest part of our crops lost. I kept a small garden of the grape cuttings you sent and a little lettuce, onions, beans, and squash near the house, but the pump went dry in August and we had to haul our water from the river. It did not rain for more than seven weeks, and the river itself nearly dried up. Soon it will be winter, and we have nothing saved but a few dried beans.

Last night, after I put Amy in her bed, I found Clayton outside, sitting on the dirt beside the house, staring into the near dark.

"What are you doing out here?" I asked him.

"Studying," he said, not moving from where he was sitting, not changing his eyes. "Studying the land I brought you to."

"Look at the sky," I told him. "Now *that* is something to study." Every night it is thick with tiny pin holes of light. There are places that look like a bowl of glittering milk got turned over, pooled, and spread across the night.

"It is something," he said, looking up. Already there were a few stars, the bright north star and three pale ones. Some nights after Amy is asleep, I spread a blanket out in the yard, and we lie there watching how many of them fall. I can get dizzy from all that light and forget where I am.

"Are you sorry you came?" he asked me.

I sat down in the dirt next to him, took his hand, and told him I didn't care about losing the money and that next year we could find a way to get water for the crops. The only thing I regret is losing Josh.

Clayton kept looking out into the night that pressed against us. "I thought I lost you," he said. "I thought you would never come back to me after I got done burying him."

I am sorry about the money John sent. Clayton has promised he will earn it back and invest it in a more certain mine, although I do not know that any of them are too sure.

Your Sister,
Abigail

January 20, 1870

Dearest Maggie,

I must thank you for the kind gifts. The apples and persimmons tasted better than anything we have here, and Amy was so pleased to have a new dress. I cannot thank you enough for the cloth and pattern. I spent all of yesterday evening cutting out my calico dress. The ones I brought from Virginia are mostly in rags.

I sent you a package by stage coach of some of the stones we have here, a small cactus I dug up for you, and a rug I bought last spring from the Indians. The baby was a boy, like yours, and we call him George Michael. He is a sweet baby and looks more like Clayton, with his dark hair, than Josh did.

Your Sister,
Abigail

April 30, 1870

Dear Maggie,

Clayton has been gone five days now, working in a new mine. This one, he assures me, will yield plenty of ore. Amy and I spend the mornings planting corn, squash, and beans, with me hoeing the long rows and Amy following behind dropping the seeds. There is a man near here with a ranch who says he can help us to get water this summer. The public acequia, a large ditch dug from the river, is not far from our land. We must dig a smaller ditch and get the water commission's order to raise the gate to let in the water. The ditches must be dug along two sides of the field and through its center. Such a lot of digging! Also, we are told we must buy a windmill and water wheel, and they are more than one hundred dollars.

I keep the baby inside, in a dark, cool corner of the house, where I made a bed for him. He is a good baby and sleeps much of the time. Last week when Clayton got back from the mines, he kissed both me and Amy, then gave a long, narrow-eyed look around the room. "Where is baby George?" he said finally.

I had laid him in his bed in a cool dark corner and stretched a piece of cloth over him to keep out the scorpions. "There," and I pointed. "Well, I will say one thing," Clayton told me. "I never have to worry that he'll be snatched up by an Indian or Mexican while I'm gone." And had to use both hands to scoop George Michael up, he has grown so.

I would spend the evenings painting the sky, which streaks with gold and every shade of purple and pink, but I have used up most of my meager supply of materials, and even if we had the money to spare, there is nowhere for me to purchase more. Instead I sit beneath all that color, mending and patching our clothing.

The afternoons are already hot, and so after lunch, Amy sleeps in the house. We had a brood of little chicks, and it is her job and delight to care for them. Before supper I read to her and try to teach her to make her letters. If I would let her, she would spend all day playing with rabbits and toads or with the Mexican children who live nearby. But I am concerned her English is suffering, since she hears only Clayton and me speak it. She is such an obedient child, and I do wish to give her every opportunity she would have in the east. But there are no schools here; indeed, I do not know of any American children living within an hour's ride.

"I like to play with the rabbits," she said one evening after hearing me discuss my concerns with Clayton. We have several we are raising now in a pen, and Amy feeds them and spends half the afternoon playing with them. She sometimes takes one out of the pen and brings it inside, carrying it around as if it were a doll. I do not know what she will say when she finds out they are for our dinner!

Your Sister,
Abigail

August 29, 1870

Dearest Maggie,

We were not able to get water for our land, and most of our crops are dried up. But there has been more rain this summer—thunderstorms that race through the valley just before sunset—and so we have some beans for drying and a little corn. I have plenty of tomatoes, green beans, and some grapes from the vines you sent.

I asked Clayton if I could visit home with the children during Christmas, but the trip by train is expensive, and unless he has more luck with the mines, we won't be able to come. I do miss you and the children. Irene and Robert must have both grown so, and I can only imagine from your descriptions what little Alex must look like. Clayton left a week ago to make the extra money we need to get our supplies for winter and has promised we can hitch the wagon and ride to Mesilla when he returns. Last year after the drought and Clayton's loss in the mines, we were unable to go. I have so looked forward to the trip. If there is enough money I will get a bolt of cloth for a new dress for me and for Amy, and I will get Mexican Christmas presents for you.

Yours,

Abigail

January 21, 1871

Dearest Maggie,

Your gifts were much appreciated. I have not had persimmons since the ones you sent last Christmas, and the shoes were needed by all of us. Amy is so used to going barefoot, she had to be shown how to button hers. Now she wears them everywhere and is proud of the buttons on them.

I am glad you liked the weavings. The carving is of olive wood and quite rare. I bought it from an Arab in Mesilla. There were all sorts of people in the market—Chinamen, Arabs, easterners, and, of course, the Mexicans. We saw every sort of vegetable and fruit and various goods for sale there also, many of which I did not know the name. There were brilliant birds in cages and richly colored cloth, porcelain figures and tea sets, if you could pay the price. The southerners have started a school and two churches. Would that we lived closer so that we could attend church and I could send Amy to school. We met a rancher who has made his fortune growing cotton. How he gets so much water I am not sure.

Clayton allowed me to purchase a new sketching pad, and I bought calico that is black-striped for dresses, and a heavy cotton for Clayton's trousers, and muslin. I will put a piece of the calico in with the letter. I have given up on bustles, the same as I did on hoops. I simply cannot get around in them.

Your Sister,
Abigail

April 15, 1871

My Dear Maggie,

Rainstorms sweep across the sky these past few weeks with the sudden sound of horses pounding over a hill or a stampede of cattle. Almost every afternoon I must call Amy inside, then we two stand at the front door, watching the thick, dark sky move towards us like a heavy cloth pulled by the hand of God. Seconds later, His fury is upon us with the pummeling of heavy drops that splatter when they hit the ground, and in an instant the world turns so thick with water that we cannot single out one drop but see only the pounding darkness as if the curtain has been drawn round us.

But it is God's blessing, also, any water that falls, even if it comes in torrents. The desert blooms wildly this spring, cacti which were dried husks all of last summer bursting with yellows, deep reds, and pinks and blues, everywhere the brilliant, exotic flowering.

There is so much rain that I have had to replant our spring crops, some several times, as the seeds wash away. But we have plenty of lettuce and greens, rows of turnips, even, and peas. I have introduced some of our varieties of vegetables to the locals, who think they are indeed good.

Clayton is away most of the time, working at the mines, and so it is Amy and I who do the planting. I carry George Michael strapped in a carrier to my back as I am planting, like a little papoose! This is a most practical arrangement, as it leaves my hands free and George Michael is content to watch us, swaying gently in his perch.

All of last week Clayton was gone, hoping he would find the vein of gold he assures me does exist. Both the water rights and a windmill must be purchased if we are to irrigate our crops, and he is hopeful the money will be forthcoming. With any luck in the mines, it will be.

We look forward to a summer, finally, when we will be able to bring in a harvest.

Your Loving Sister,
Abigail

June 1, 1871

Dear Maggie,

There have been days these past few months when I have wished the mines and the gold and copper, whatever comes out of them, into oblivion. When Clayton returns from them he is most often in a rage, for every mine he invests in fails. Three days ago he rode up just before supper and threw his bags on the floor. He was standing in the doorway—all dark with the sun behind him—and Amy ran to me, saying she was afraid. "That's right, child," Clayton told her. "Run from me. Wherever I go, there is no good comes of it."

"Forget the mines," I said to him after we had eaten supper. "If we can get more water for the crops, we can try farming. You said yourself the land is fertile."

Clayton shook his head and laughed. "All we need is water," he said, throwing his hands up as if the only way we could get it would be from God Himself. Indeed, Maggie, some days it does seem this is true. There has been no rain for ten days, and already, this early in the summer, after such a wet spring, the ground is dry.

But I must keep hope, so I grabbed one of his hands between mine. It was thick, and rougher than when we lived in Virginia. "We have the water," I told him. "We only have to get it up here."

"All right," he said, but looked as if he had given up

making things work here. "I'll go tomorrow and see about the water rights. We still need money for a windmill and a pump. But if I pull out all my money, we might scrape together enough." He stopped talking and looked straight at me. "It will mean quitting the mines."

I almost smiled. I am overtired, Maggie, of him being gone days at a time. "The seeds are nearly in," I told him. "Amy and I will start digging the ditches." We had watered the garden near the house, but the corn and cotton and beans need water from the river.

"It is what I came here for," Clayton said, so quietly I had to stop thinking to hear him. "The mines are what I came here for."

I had nothing to say to that and went to call Amy from the yard, where she was splashing cool water on herself at the pump.

Clayton left the next morning to collect his money. He is not back yet. I spent all day with Amy in the field, hitting the ground with the hoe, breaking up the dirt for planting or digging an irrigation ditch. I promised her we will buy more chickens and rabbits with the money that is left over. She wanted to know if we could get a cow for milk and butter, and I told her she would have to help walk it every day to the river, where there is enough grass. I thank God for sparing her, she is such a good girl.

Your Sister,
Abigail

September 12, 1871

Dear Maggie,

I have not had the heart to write to you all of this. Clayton got what money he could out of the mines, but we did not have enough after buying the windmill to purchase the water rights. All during the dry summer, we sat with our windmill and ditches partly dug, watching our crops burn up. I was afraid to put water on the patch near the house for fear that the pump might go dry, and we lost even the grape vines. Feed corn is so high this year we cannot get enough for the chickens, but they and the rabbits are the only food we have.

I went out at sunset tonight and walked to the river. The sky, which is like a huge bowl that fits over everything, was streaked with red and purple. The colors spread across the mountains and got all through me until the whole world was blazing. I cannot understand how land that is this beautiful can be this hard.

Mr. Peerson, who has a big ranch near here, says it took him three years to get water and we should not give up, the land is too good. He gets so much cotton he has to pay Mexicans to help pick it. I nearly asked would he pay us, but that would not have been seemly.

I must confess, I am of different minds about your news. Of course, I am glad for you that John has made such a success of his store, but as I am sure it means you are less likely to join us in New Mexico, I am also saddened.

Yours,
Abigail

January 29, 1872

Dearest Maggie,

Clayton is gone now except one day a week, freighting supplies to the mining camps. He does not talk about speculating anymore. There seems to be surer money in freighting.

You say that I must ask myself why I came, that I must regret the trip since our life here has not met with success. I can only tell you my life seems as it should be. Each morning I peer out our narrow window and see mountains, which cut into the deep-blue sky. They have sharp, clean lines, and in the winter they are partly white with snow. I cannot imagine my life elsewhere.

Mr. Peerson is an interesting man. He came here eight years ago from Texas to establish a ranch. His wife died that first winter, but he has stayed on alone, learning the complicated methods of irrigation and raising cattle and sheep. He has sometimes gone for months without conversing with another Anglo, as we are called here, but that does not seem to bother him.

Several years ago he was hired by the government as an Indian interpreter, and he speaks many of their languages. There is a story that his wife was dark, that he met her while living with a tribe to learn its language, but I do not believe it. A few weeks ago Mr. Peerson's nephew, who is a doctor, came to stay with him. I am much relieved to have a doctor staying so close by. Last week, when Dr. Mayfield heard that Amy had cut her foot on a rough board, he came over and offered to look at the wound and put a fresh dressing on it. He did all this and gave me some syrup for George Michael, who has a belly ache now and again, and he would not take any of the chickens I offered him to carry back to Mr. Peerson. We have good neighbors here, so do not despair for me.

Your Sister,
Abigail

April 29, 1872

Dearest Maggie,

The desert is in bloom. It is still strange for me to see the hard, thorny cacti covered with delicate blossoms. The prickly pears in our yard have deep-pink blossoms the size of roses. I look into their thick, spiraling petals and cannot find myself. On long afternoons when Clayton is gone, I get out my sketching paper and try to draw them. The cottonwoods near the river will flower soon. In early summer they are covered with downy white flakes and delicate leaves.

Dr. Mayfield has decided to stay on through the summer. He tells me he has fallen in love with the desert. Clayton took him riding last weekend up into the mountains, where they saw several antelopes. The evening they returned, I left Amy and George Michael with a reliable Mexican woman, and Clayton and I rode out to Mr. Peerson's ranch for dinner.

After Mr. Peerson's wife died, he hired a Mexican woman, who does all his cooking. The food was very spicy, as she mixes hot red peppers in everything. There were dishes of corn, rice, and beans, and she cooked pieces of chicken and served them with a spicy sauce. Clayton and I drank several glasses of water with this meal, but Clayton said he would like to have more of the hot peppers. Mr. Peerson promised to send over some seeds. There was fine china on the table, and the floors are all wooden and covered with Mexican rugs.

After dinner, Clayton and the men played cards. Another couple was visiting from one of the mining towns, touring the area. The lady wanted me to play cribbage with her and smoke. She was dressed in bright red and blue taffeta, a fancy dress with a bustle. She had a loud voice and seemed to find everything quite funny, such a disappointment, as she is the sole female I have met since leaving the camps.

Clayton says we will have money enough to purchase water rights by next month. He has filed a petition with the water commissioner, and we are waiting for their reply. Meanwhile, Amy and I are digging more ditches. She has taught George Michael how to feed the chickens, and he spends much of his day trying to chase after them. We will plant a small crop and hope to keep it watered this year!

Your Loving Sister,
Abigail

August 4, 1872

Dear Maggie,

At the last minute the water commissioner raised the price we were to pay for water rights, and we were unable to purchase them. But we did manage to use a few of the ditches, pumping rain water we collected and what we could carry. There was more rain than usual in July, and so we have a harvest of sorts.

Each evening I put the children to bed just before sunset and join Clayton in the field. We pull corn cobs from their stalks or yank bean plants from the ground until dark. The sun sets in the mountains to the west of us, streaking the sky with every shade of red and pink, turning the mountains a deep purple. The only sounds are the rustling of the corn or beans and the low hum of insects. Sometimes it seems the world has stopped. Then Clayton calls to me and says we should go to bed so that we can start again at sunrise.

The beans and corn and potatoes will last us much of the winter. There are also tomatoes, grapes, cucumbers, and squash. Amy goes out to the garden near the house just after she wakes, sits on the dirt, and eats whatever she can reach.

Dr. Mayfield returned recently from a town in northern New Mexico, where he is thinking about setting up his practice. He said it is a growing town with plenty of people, but he is in love with this valley, the river and the mountains. Yesterday evening he came by with a string of fish he had caught, which were most delicious. Clayton says this is the place for him even if the mines did fail. He and Dr. Mayfield have planned a hunting trip next weekend if the rest of our crops are in. There are all kinds of antelopes, fox, deer, wild sheep, and rabbits in the mountains. You must come for a long visit, and soon, now that our ranch is beginning to prosper!

Your Sister,
Abigail

Between Earth and Sky

September 19, 1872

Dearest Maggie,

Last week Clayton left with a wagon load of goods for the mines some miles north of here. He has been offered employment there and will most likely stay on an additional month to earn the wage they are paying out, which is good. Mr. John Deering, who has taken a piece of land about ten miles from here, rode out with Clayton to get work. Clayton has assured me he will send word once he arrives. If the work is good and he intends to stay the winter, I will join him with the children next month.

Mr. Deering's wife is anxious to go and see the camps, for she imagines they will be more exciting than living on a farm in the desert. I have tried to describe the type of excitement that fills the camps, but she persists in her curiosity about them. If her husband would let her, I believe she would leave their house and move into a tent tomorrow. She is friendly, if a little naive. She does not believe a lady should learn to use a gun and counts on her eleven-year-old son to protect her. Ten miles is a long way to go with two small children. Still, I enjoy our talk of dress patterns and chicken raising and schooling. I have already made the journey several times.

Days pass when I see no one but the Mexican women who live near by. They are heavy-set, all of them that I have met, and dark-skinned, with black hair and eyes. They speak very little English. Mrs. Deering complains she hired a Mexican woman as a housekeeper and found her unreliable. She says she has heard they are worse than the Negroes. When the Mexican field workers get tired of their work, they just get on their horses and ride off, even if it is early in the afternoon. At the end of the week, they still expect a full week's pay, and it is hard arguing with them when they spit out streams of Spanish.

Our only other visitor is Dr. Mayfield, who has been kind enough to ride over every few days to check on us. Yesterday he helped Amy catch a horned toad to keep as a pet. She has become fond of goat's milk mixed with her porridge in the mornings and recently took over the milking of Sybil, the goat, a gentle animal who would never bite but sometimes attempts to wander away before Amy has finished. Last night I made a sweet potato pie, and we ate it with a cup of the milk.

I heard from Sally recently; both she and Bea send letters at least twice a year. Sally has two boys now along with Rachel and reports they are all healthy. Her husband has gone north for a few months to earn money logging, while she and her little ones live with the Sterns until his return.

I have nearly given up writing to Mother, as my letters are never answered. Tell her that both of the children are well and that our crops have met with some success. I will send you a few of the seeds from the peppers we dried!

Your Loving Sister,
Abigail

74

November 4, 1872

Dearest Maggie,

George Michael has been sick three days now. His throat is all red and he has a bright rash all along his arms and back. Dr. Mayfield fears it is scarlet fever. He stayed with us part of the afternoon yesterday, giving every kind of medicine, and would take nothing for it.

I still have no word from Clayton, and it has been two months. I told Dr. Mayfield my fear that Clayton is hurt somewhere, and he said John Deering got back a few days ago and he would ride over to ask what the news is. I cannot see why Clayton would be gone this long with no word sent back, but there is every kind of danger on the open road through the desert, and the mining towns are so full of killings that many go unnoticed.

Your Sister,
Abigail

November 7, 1872

Dearest Maggie,

At just an hour past dawn, little George passed the crisis, and I know now, Sister, that he will live. Yesterday evening I was sure we would lose him. His temperature had risen, and he was so weak he could not drink anything. Dr. Mayfield stayed the night, and I am certain George Michael would not be alive this morning if Dr. Mayfield had not been here. He had a bottle of syrup and gave it to George Michael liberally, also quinine. All night I rubbed his arms and legs with alcohol and applied mustard packs, until the fever was drawn out.

Shortly after the fever broke, I walked outside to wash the used linens at the pump and fell down on my knees to thank God. When I stood again, my hands and knees were coated with red dust, as we have not had rain for several weeks. But I did not care. I wiped my face with this earth, grateful that it had not taken another child from me, unsure whether or not my husband is buried somewhere in it.

When I turned towards the house, I saw that Dr. Mayfield stood beside the door, watching me. He took my hands and placed them against his shirt so that he too was covered with dust. I pressed myself against him and we two stood like that, touching, as the air turned from darkness to a pale, palpable gray.

I should not have kissed him, should not have let myself stay there with him all that time it took the sun to stain the horizon. I did not mean to, Maggie. You must not tell a word of this. It was my exhaustion. I could not stand to lose another of my babies and Clayton all at once.

I do not remember who was the first to pull away. By then, the mountains were visible against the pale, wide sky, and the earth that lay all around us had turned yellow and brown.

Your Sister,
Abigail

December 4, 1872

Dear Maggie,

It has been three months, and still no word of Clayton. Dr. Mayfield has ridden to all the nearby ranches and inquired about him, but no one knows what has happened. John Deering has said that Clayton went on to another mine where they were digging. Much of the area is said to be rich in coal. I wait and pray for news.

I do not understand myself anymore. I have continued to encourage Dr. Mayfield's visits. I cannot seem to turn him away. Do you think it possible there is another being in me, another self who acts so impulsively without my approval?

Yesterday I left the children with Mr. Peerson's housekeeper and rode out towards the mountains with Thomas, on the pretext of finding a miner who is reported to live there and asking if he has heard of Clayton's whereabouts.

The wind bit into our faces, and I felt the large muscles of the horse straining under me as we rode across the desert. Clayton would have insisted we take the wagon, but on horseback I felt I had been let loose somehow in all that wind from every earthly concern. I thought of the girl I was who rode sometimes all morning across the fields through all that swirl of green and blue, and how I wanted to become a musician or an artist or travel to Europe to study. Was it the war that turned us around so, filled us with practical concerns?

Maggie, Dr. Mayfield came west not to earn out a living but because he had to see it for himself: the plains, the mountains, the desert, buffaloes and Indians, the fields of flowers, the red and purple cliffs. He is filling note pads with writing and sketches. I have seen them, the charcoal drawings and those he colored with pastels. How drab and ordinary Clayton's and my plans for earning a living out of the desert seem next to his. How like the young girl in me still (and oh, I thought she was gone after Father and David's deaths and half the boys we knew in Gaten County) to not refuse a ride to the mountains or the loan of a book of prints.

We did not find the miner's house, but returned all the same before dusk, having built a small fire on which to heat our lunch and lain in each other's arms. Thomas has told me that if Clayton does not return by next month, he will ride north and try to find him or get word of what has happened. Mrs. Deering tells of a woman left alone in the desert one year waiting for word which never came from her husband. Finally, she gave up her claim and took her children farther west to live with her sister in California.

I can imagine her there, how she stayed on week after week despite fear of attack by some bushwhacker or outlaw, afraid to leave, to break off all chance that she would hear of her husband. I wonder how she managed the cold and food for her children and keeping the stock alive. I wonder how she managed.

I am yours,
Abigail

January 2, 1873

Dear Maggie,

The Christmas holiday passed with no news of Clayton's whereabouts. It is almost four months now since he rode away to work in the mines. He had planned to be gone one month at most before sending for us, but I have heard nothing. The aggravation of not knowing is nearly too much to bear. If he has been trapped in some mine shaft deep inside the earth or shot at night along some roadside, I wonder if I will hear of it. There are stories of bones found in the desert, picked clean, with no way of knowing what outlaw or poor lone traveler they belonged to.

Mr. and Mrs. Deering called on me and the children Christmas afternoon, insisting we ride back to their homestead for dinner. Mr. Peerson and Dr. Mayfield were there also, along with Mr. Peerson's brother and his wife and son. I had received your letter the previous week, and acting on your good advice I had told Dr. Mayfield I could not see him again until I know for certain what has become of Clayton. An argument had ensued, in which he called me "cruel" and "unnatural," but I held to my resolution.

You can imagine my position, then, forced to sit at Christmas dinner with him among the other company, but the meal passed pleasantly; he is a gentleman. After a dinner of venison and squash, breads and pudding, there was a small exchange of gifts. I had brought little with me, a piece of embroidery for Mrs. Deering. The children all received candy sticks, and I accepted the drawing pad from Dr. Mayfield, as it would have been awkward to refuse it.

The day after Christmas the wind was so fierce I dared not go outside. By noon it was nearly dark, and sand rattled the glass, piling up against the windows. To calm my fears, I took out my new pad and made sketches of the children and the mountains. I even drew a scene from the mining camps and a picture of our wagon headed westward across the prairie.

The next day, after the wind had stopped and the sky turned blue and still again, I took the drawings I had made out into the light and saw what a mass of confusion some of them were, filled with thick dark lines. Dr. Mayfield came that afternoon to see if the wind had destroyed us, and when he caught sight of a drawing I had made of the mountain, asked if he could have it. I did not think to refuse him after all he has done for us.

The next day he came again, and the one after that. And so, Maggie, my resolve to do as you advised has weakened. Next week he has promised to ride across the mountains and look for Clayton.

Your Sister,

Abigail

February 7, 1873

Dear Maggie,

A month has passed since I last wrote, but it seems to me more than a year. Thomas had planned to ride over the mountains in search of news about Clayton, but we had a snowstorm the second week of January, and the mountains became impassable. I may have to wait for spring before I can learn of Clayton's fate.

81

Thomas has been our faithful guardian throughout the cold, carrying a wagon load of wood from Mr. Peerson's in the worst of the snow. Then one night last week, after there were rumors of an Indian uprising, he and Mr. Peerson brought us in the wagon to Mr. Peerson's ranch, where we spent three comfortable nights on feather mattresses under thick quilts and comforters.

More than once I asked them to let me do the cooking, cleaning, or mending as payment for their kindness, but they would not hear me and instead spent hours entertaining us with stories of their adventures. Thomas has traveled across the mountains of Colorado and seen one of the last herds of buffalo. Last spring he was led through a canyon filled with unusual rock formations by an Indian guide. Mr. Peerson told of the months he spent living with a tribe in Texas. There was a man bit by a rattlesnake who was cured of it by an Indian doctor, and Mr. Peerson witnessed several of the Indian dances. He was quite impressed with the chief, who he said was more intelligent than most white men. The world is so much larger than Stillwater, Maggie, and at times I cannot get enough of it.

But this evening I am alone, now that the children have fallen asleep. The wind still rages, and I feel it sitting as close to the stove as I dare. This is the first cold winter since we arrived in the southwest, and it seems fate has sent it to keep Clayton and me apart. Sometimes the world is full of ominous possibilities, and I imagine Clayton's death in a mining accident or a shoot-out or in the cold desert again and again.

Thomas has asked what I will do if we cannot discover what happened to Clayton, how long I will wait to hear of him. I cannot answer. A life with Thomas would be filled with all that is exciting. He wants to travel throughout the territory and into Mexico. His family is a prominent one, Maggie, back east, and he was graduated from the best of schools. He fought as a medic with the north during the war, but I do not care anymore. The desert obliterates old divisions.

As soon as it is possible to travel over the mountains, Thomas has promised me he will find out what has become of Clayton. Sister, you are my sole confidante. Do not relate to Mother or Aunt Celia any of what I write.

Yours,
Abigail

March 2, 1873

Dear Maggie,

This morning Thomas rode out across the mountains to search for Clayton. I do not know what to hope for. In truth, I can only hope that I will learn what has happened to him, for not knowing has become almost unbearable. If Clayton has died, I have agreed to stay with Mr. Peerson under the guise of housekeeper until further plans can be made. The children are fond of Thomas; George Michael knows more of him than he remembers of his father. Under the circumstances, it would not be necessary to wait long to remarry.

Your letters urge faith and discretion, and you are right, I must believe that life's unfolding has some meaning and that I will soon see clearly the direction I must take. If Clayton lives, Thomas has said he will leave the territory at once. We will endeavor to forget one another. Only Mr. Peerson and you, my dear sister, know of our circumstances, and Mr. Peerson has pledged his secrecy.

Pray for me,
Abigail

April 15, 1873

Dear Maggie,

Last week Clayton was returned to us. Dr. Mayfield located him just outside a mining camp where he was staying with a friend of Mr. Stone's. He had taken up work at a newer mine for higher pay, sending word that he would be back at the end of two months, but neither that letter nor the messages he would send later reached us. Just a few days before he was to ride home, he was injured.

It is his back, Maggie, and I do not see how he will ever be the same again. He is all bent over and cannot walk or sit or ride for very long. If Dr. Mayfield had not found him, he would not have been able to come back over the mountains for some time. Dr. Mayfield says the back should mend but that Clayton may never regain the strength he once had.

Since his return, Clayton spends much of the day lying in bed, watching the children play through the open doorway. George Michael hardly seems to remember his own father and holds my skirts when Clayton reaches out for him. Dr. Mayfield has gone east. He has said he might return to the territory to open a practice north of here in a larger town. I do not imagine I will see him again.

We have enough food and money to get through this month and the next, but I do not know what we will do come summer. Clayton will not talk of returning to Virginia; in truth, he talks very little. I cannot imagine that he will be able to work for the mines. I do not know what will become of us.

Your Sister,
Abigail

85

$\mathcal{C}hapter$ 3

May 22, 1873

Dearest Maggie,

You asked in your letter about Clayton's health. His back is mending, slowly, but he stays in bed much of the day and will not talk with me about what we should do come summer. Dr. Mayfield told us that if Clayton continued bed rest, with a set of prescribed exercises, he should be able to stand and perhaps walk again by the end of the summer. He recommended the baths north of here, near the mines. These are hot pools of water, thick with minerals and said to cure nearly everything—rheumatism, all manner of physical debility, and spinal diseases, including paralysis.

Our water rights have been contested, and I am afraid our hard work of digging the ditches was done in vain. We recently got word that we have lost the rights unless we pay more in water taxes than even Mr. Peerson with all his acres pays. I do not see how this could happen, except that we have heard almost everyone on the board speaks Spanish, and I suppose they went against us.

My hope is that Clayton will be well enough by late June to travel and will agree to go north. The Deerings plan to travel north also, as the land is easier to farm, and they would like to start a small ranch.

I understand your meaning in your letter when you write that I should no longer mention what is past. I am sure there are times when Aunt Celia and even Mother request to read my letters. Do what you think best with those I have sent during the last year; dispose of them if need be. I will say no more.

You ask me also to return to Virginia, where you can be of help. Believe me, Maggie, when I say what I long for most is to feel myself in your sturdy arms and hear your calm, sensible voice. But I have lived on this desert for five years now. It is a hard place to make a home, but it is also beautiful. I do not know how else to say this, except that my heart, my very soul, has become one with it. In the spring I am wild with the deep green of the cottonwoods and the cactus's exotic blossoming. Throughout summer, it is my own self that is dried and parched and windblown. The sky here is like no other, and Maggie, its bright wide bowl is the lining of my soul.

Perhaps you are right. My "desert love," as you call it, may have grown from fear. As you say, it has taken one of my children and perhaps the health of my husband. Aunt Celia's letters describe Mother's anger over the lack of responsibility she believes I have taken for Amy and George Michael. I suppose you are right and she would forgive all were I to return, but can I do so, in defeat? And, Maggie, we have little money. You have written yourself that John's business is just large enough for him and his brother. I am afraid our lives in Virginia would not be any easier.

Please try to understand the sense of this, dear sister. Do not blame me too much.

Abigail

June 10, 1873

Dear Maggie,

We set off in a few days. Clayton moves about a little more freely now, and I have spent the last two months repairing the wagon and purchasing two good mules to pull it. Amy has been such a help with George Michael and the packing of our belongings. I am hopeful we will be able to find schooling for her. When I read of Irene and Robert's progress, I get discouraged that Amy will never advance the way she should with just the simple knowledge I have taught her at home.

The Deerings, one other family, and several single travelers will compose our group, led by Mr. Shumway, who has had experience as a scout. We will follow the Rio Grande into northern New Mexico and with any luck should be settled by summer's end.

Be assured, I will write as soon as I know where we will settle. And I will hope that you will forgive me. You are right, I suppose, in saying that last winter Clayton would have agreed to move back to Virginia. I cannot imagine anything that he would have chosen to fight me on. I pray that you will find it in yourself to accept this.

Your Sister,
Abigail

September 21, 1873

My Dear Maggie,

We are settled on a small piece of land near the town of North Valverde, along the mountain range. The desert is not all dry sand and rock and clay. There are many places where a river or creek runs through the land, turning it green with vegetation. Cottonwoods, willows, and oak trees are common in such areas. In the spring and early summer, flowers bloom in abundance, and anything which one plants in the wet, sandy soil is likely to thrive.

Maggie, our land is just such a place as I have described. We have purchased land in a valley created by two rivers. The water runs through our land, and we are free to plant on its banks. The property was more dear because of this, but we know well the value of land that is near water. Clayton worries, as we have spent everything to purchase it; I know we have done what is right and will prosper for years to come. When I saw the green of the cottonwood leaves and prairie grass side by side with the different shades of brown and red that mark the desert-like mountains, all of it covered by the blue of the sky, I knew we were home and that my heart had found its place.

We have bought the land from the Spanish-speaking people who settled here more than a hundred years ago. Water rights come with the land purchase, but we will need to dig ditches from the main acequia to irrigate the fields. The area is quite mixed with Spaniards, Indians, white settlers, and some Mexicans, the majority of the landowners being Spanish. I feel I have entered a foreign land. Indeed, one hears all kinds of languages spoken, and there are few who speak clear English. But the Deerings have bought land not too far north of us, and there are several other settlers from the east in this valley.

The evening after we moved into the house, which consists of a dirt floor and clay walls with a wooden roof, I noticed several dark, shadowy figures moving past the windows. I was so frightened I hardly felt my feet touching the soft dirt as I crept across the floor and slipped my finger around the trigger of the shotgun. When I opened the door, I saw them—four Indians, three of them squaws and one an old man. They had opened a bin beside the house. I assumed they were looking for food. After I gave them each a hominy cake left from our supper, they disappeared into the night like smoke.

I am thankful that we have enough flour and corn to see us through most of the winter and that we have our little sheet-iron stove. We had to sell our goat and chickens, but we carried a beehive with us under the wagon. At the springs where we stopped so that Clayton could take advantage of their healing properties, we heard of all kinds of miracles— a lame child who walked without his crutches after just four days, and there was a woman cured of tuberculosis. After two weeks, Clayton was much the same, but by the time we reached the valley, he was improved and able to walk. He claims it was all the stumbling he did through the desert air, but I am not sure that it wasn't the springs.

Oh, Maggie, please do be happy for me. And send us all good wishes for our new beginning.

Abigail

Karen Osborn

December 11, 1873

Dear Maggie,

Each day here in our desert home is thick with all that is new and unusual for us to see and hear. I have grown so used to hearing Spanish that many words are familiar to me, but the Indian words sound as if they were blown here from some foreign place. I suppose, in actuality, it is Clayton and myself that have arrived unexpectedly, whisked, it seems, by the wind across the sand and the clay-covered earth.

The houses are made mostly of adobe, which we are told is practical, as they stay cool despite the heat in the summer. Many of the mud huts hang great strings of red peppers on their doors in the fall. There are large flocks of sheep near the mountains, and the rivers descend like threads of silver.

The Indians grow corn, wheat, pumpkins, squash, melons, and even grapes. The women carry their babies on boards against their backs, and they carry water by balancing large earthen pots on their heads. I saw a woman making tortillas, which look like thick, large pancakes. Tomorrow is a great feast day for the Catholics. We are told that between the Spanish people and the Indians, there will be an abundance of whiskey and dancing.

Yesterday, despite the cold, I scrubbed two tubs full of clothes. I have made myself a pair of bloomers out of heavy cotton, which come almost to my ankles. It would make sense to wear shorter skirts here, but I have not been able to convince myself to do so.

Last month there was a rattlesnake in our front yard. It came close to striking George, who was sitting in the dirt with a pile of sticks he had made. Before I knew it, I had thrown a large rock at its head. The thing was stunned long enough for me to grab hold of the ax which was nearby and chop off its head. Later Clayton skinned it, and now we have its shell hanging on the wall just inside our door, a reminder of my bravery.

When we travel up into the mountains, there are no roads, only the peaks, which we have named after the presidents, to guide us. Not far from our house is a mesa, a mountain which is long and flat across the top. When I open my front door, I can see it stretching across a length of sky, cutting its straight, certain line above the horizon.

Here is a letter I got from Sally last summer. I expect you know about Adam and Grey going off to Colorado, but the rest may be news to you.

Your Sister,
Abigail

July 29, 1873

Dear Abigail,

I had another boy, born last month, a big strong baby like William, and I called him Matthew. I am staying here in the hills with Rachel and the boys, with a family called the Harmons, while Roger is gone these two or three months to earn a living out of those mines. I would be so glad if he would give them up like your Clayton. If there is nothing in these ones, he says he will, and then we can live in town in our own house. There is a need for men that can do carpentry, and I feel sure we would be all right.

My duties here are the cleaning of the house and cooking for the five Harmons and the four men who work for them. There is plenty of variety of vegetables here, and so I invent all kinds of recipes, like squash and green pepper pie, which we ate last night. There are two girls for Rachel to play with, and if we are still here in a month's time I will send her off to school with the others. She is learning hard work at a young age—hauling buckets of laundry, scrubbing and cleaning, caring for the baby and Will. I would like to see her get some sort of education before she is grown.

Do you think often of Virginia? I do and long to go back, though there is nothing really to go back to in the way of making a living, as Roger has said to me too many times. It is awful how I miss my mother. Nearly most of my family is there still. But did you hear that Adam and Grey went to Colorado? I guess they will work the mines. Mother *says they are bound for adventure and may come the rest of the way across to California. Wouldn't that be grand?*

I do think of you often, Abigail. Perhaps we will see one another again.

Your Sally

February 7, 1874

Dear Maggie,

We had snow last week, the most Amy could remember ever having seen. The world got whiter and whiter all morning, and by afternoon the tree limbs and our house were heavy with it. Clayton stayed inside by the stove, as his back was hurting again, but Amy and I bundled up against the cold and went out. I felt like a child again, running through all that whiteness. When the sky turned a hard, bright blue, everything was glittering. We fashioned a rabbit out of snow for George Michael, who was watching from the window.

Maggie, I hate to write to you to ask for anything after Clayton lost John's money and after all you have given us. But I can think of nowhere else to turn. Clayton's father has given all he can, and we are still quite low on supplies. I do not see how we can get through the winter. Thirty or forty dollars would be enough, as soon we shall be able to plant. Maggie, I am asking for a loan. Know that I will return the money by next fall, and soon we will repay John the money lost to the mines.

I am your thankful, indebted sister,
Abigail

March 1, 1874

Dear Maggie,

I am unsure of when I will be able to post this letter, as we have had a recent snowfall and Clayton tells me it will be a few days at least before we can reach the main roads, but I feel I must write despite this to thank you for the generous loan you sent. It arrived a few days ago and is none too soon, as we have depleted our stores of nearly everything, including flour and sugar. I do not know how we would have survived the next month if not for your generosity. As soon as the roads have melted enough for passage, Clayton will take the wagon to the nearest store and purchase enough to see us through for another month. We will certainly be in need of these extra provisions, as winter has lasted much longer than we planned on.

When the snow is melted, we will begin planting. We

are told root crops do quite well here in the spring, including carrots and turnips, and many of the farmers plant spinach and lettuce. I have already marked off a large kitchen garden, enough, I hope, to provide all of us with something freshly grown during the spring months.

This summer we plan to use the acequia to irrigate. Each landowner is given a specified time during which he can raise the gate, allowing water to flow into his ditches, and various penalties result if a landowner is caught raising the gate when it is not his time to do so. Still, if someone upstream were to use our share of the water, it would be difficult to prove his dishonesty. Señor López, from whom we purchased our land, is a large and powerful landowner who farms a nearby tract of land, and we are counting on his influence to protect our water rights. But in a drought, as Clayton has pointed out to me, there is no way to know how one's neighbors will act.

Your Sister,
Abigail

August 5, 1874

Dear Maggie,

We have had enough alfalfa to sell some, and so I am sending the money you kindly loaned us last winter. We planted nearly an acre in alfalfa, first leveling the ground, then dividing it into squares with raised borders, finally digging the ditches to carry the water. Maintaining these ditches is time-consuming, but well worth it. We have had four good cuttings in one season.

This past month Clayton made some money speculating on the mines south of here. He insists on taking half his earnings and investing them on a new site. I have tried to persuade him against speculation, but he will not hear me, and so I count this money gone. We spent part of what was left on the purchase of two buff-colored mules. There is enough remaining for Amy's school tuition and her board for the winter.

The only church nearby is a Catholic chapel. It has a courtyard with all kinds of statues painted so that the place looks nearly like a circus. The Virgin Mary is a bright blue, as brilliant a shade as the sky (indeed, I have heard a woman refer to her painted robes as the sky's mirror), and her skin is not cream colored but a darker shade, with the red of an autumn leaf or the sienna of clay. The folds of her dress and the features of her face are nearly primitive in their design, angular and harsh as if the artist did not know how to mold the lines. The feet are wide and the toes thicker than human toes. The hands also do not have the graceful curves we are accustomed to seeing on fine works of art.

By your last letter I see we are both to be delivered soon. I expect mine to come near Christmas. Amy will attend school, boarding in Santa Fe for the winter with the family of one of the other children in the school. While I have longed to send her, I know I shall miss her terribly, and even at the age of eleven, she seems young to be away at school. During the many days of Clayton's long absences, I spoke to no one but Amy. Sometimes it seems we are of the same mind, and I thank God that after losing Josh, I have been able to keep my first born.

Your grateful and devoted sister,
Abigail

December 6, 1874

Dear Maggie,

I have sent you a package. You should receive notice of it in a week or two, as I sent it by railroad. There is nothing of too great an expense in it, just an Indian basket and a few trifles from the southwest which you may find amusing.

This year we are well prepared for the season, with grains, dried beans, and the vegetables and fruit we have dried or preserved. We have a large quantity of wood cut, and Clayton has been on a few profitable hunting expeditions. Many of the people here raise hogs, goats, and chickens, and as soon as Clayton is able, we will build a barn so that we can raise our own livestock.

George has had a cough, and I have given him plenty of red pepper tea and wrapped his throat and chest in flannel. Clayton goes to town next week to bring Amy back to us, and Mrs. Deering has offered to come and stay. My hope is that the baby will wait until Clayton's and Amy's return, but if not, Mrs. Deering is of a sensible mind and will be of great help.

Will Mother not write to us, even at Christmas time? You write that she is full of concern about my condition. I sent her another letter, all but begging her to reply, more than four weeks ago now, and still I have received nothing. How is it you can say that I am the prideful one?

Your Repentant Sister,
Abigail

January 3, 1875

Dearest Maggie,

I received your letter and celebrated your news of Susan's arrival. Margaret Anne was born just before Christmas. She has hair dark as yours and blue eyes. I hope you are pleased by the name. If I cannot have my sister here in the flesh, I will have you here in spirit. She is a sweet baby but very colicky. I do not know if it is the water or maybe the drafts make her stomach cramp. But do not worry about her; she has the strongest set of lungs you have ever heard!

Amy was here for three whole weeks. She has learned reading, writing, and sewing and is quite the young lady. George Michael pestered to get her to chase jack rabbits, but she would not. She was such a help with the new baby, and every evening we spent reading together from a book of poems she had been given by her teacher. I shall miss her this long winter.

You would hardly know our house was the same shack we moved into a year ago. There is one big room made mostly of clay bricks, and we have put in a six-pane window and a wooden door. I put straw under the rag carpet Amy and I wove last summer and tacked it down. Our bed is on a platform, the curtains are put up, and Clayton got a store-bought rocker and two more chairs to go with our table. I trimmed the shelves Clayton made with newspapers cut in fancy patterns. With the stove going, we are quite snug, a far piece from last winter, when our walls gleamed with a sheet of ice and the air itself was nearly crystallized with frost.

Last week our neighbor Señora Teresa Martínez took me inside the Catholic church. It is small and built of clay bricks, lined inside with crude wooden benches that are the pews. There were a number of statues inside, similar to those in the courtyard, except that they are actually dressed, the same way you would dress up a doll, in lace and bright satin. A statue of the body of Jesus had been made and placed in a glass casket which stands along one of the walls. The figure was quite realistic, complete with gashes and blood.

Señora Teresa told a strange story about the man who sculpted it. As he worked on the statue, his feet bled from mysterious holes, which could not be healed. It became his wish to live long enough to finish his sculpture for the church, and when he did he prepared to die. At that moment the holes closed over, and a red rose bush grew instantly on the ground where the last of his blood had fallen.

Our Spanish neighbors wave to us, shouting greetings as we ride by in the wagon, but I have not been able to converse much with them. I do not understand their beliefs in miracles and curses, devils and witches. It seems they celebrate frequently, and we have heard that any wedding, baptism, or saint's day is an excuse for a fiesta or a dance.

Several Protestants besides ourselves have settled in the valley. Mrs. Porter lives with her husband and two boys not far from here, and the Deerings are establishing their ranch less than a day's ride north. Mrs. Porter came to call on me last week, and we discussed setting up a sewing circle, even if it is just the two of us in attendance.

Indians still come to the house, mostly to beg for food, and it is likely if we have any visitors on a cold winter day it will be them. They go through the scraps I put out for the rabbits; they are really quite sad. Last fall Clayton and I visited a small group of them that live near here, and I must say that the majority of them are very industrious; I think these beggars are but a small portion of the entire Indian people. They have plentiful gardens and weave rugs and blankets from the wool of the sheep they raise.

You must write and give the news about everyone. I have a letter recently from Aunt Celia but still none from Mother. It seems as if Mother has lost all affection for me. Aunt Celia writes that my decision not to return to Virginia two years ago was a great disappointment to Mother and that she refuses to open my letters herself but seems to listen if Aunt Celia reads them to her. Do I no longer exist for her? Can she be so cruel? Aunt Celia advises me to bring the children east for a visit. If I were able to manage the trip, could amends be made? Would she allow me to return to the southwest without resenting my leaving of Virginia all over again? I am afraid her animosity would be doubled.

I am your loving sister,
Abigail

May 2, 1875

Dear Maggie,

I must thank you for your comforting words about Mother. I suppose it is her love for me which makes it so difficult for her to accept my leaving. I will continue to write to her, as you advise, even if she does give the appearance of turning away my letters.

We have had a wet spring, thunderstorms driven out of the mountains across the valley, the entire sky a churning pot with the explosion of clouds and brilliant, sharp lines of lightning. Then, as soon as the rain stopped, the sky was swept clean. The river and ditches became so full with water, gushing and running with a swift current, that several times a week Clayton had to ride out to repair a bank or remove branches and whole trees which had been knocked loose by the force of the water.

Last month a Spanish boy drowned trying to drag a tree from the river. After Clayton helped to retrieve his body from the tangled branches, he attended the boy's wake, a strange affair, with the boy laid out in the main room and much drinking, eating, and crying going on all around him. There was a guitar and singing. Clayton swears some of the sounds were unearthly, strange moans, the screech of some animal, and there was a gust of wind that came and pulled at the boy's hair; all this while the doors and windows remained closed.

"It was as if there were ghosts," he told me. All night there was an owl just outside our window, and I do not think either one of us slept through its queer, dark sounds.

Doña Romero, an old woman who was born in this valley and learned to speak some English years ago from a missionary, claims that the excess of water so early in the season forebodes a dry summer. "Too much, too early," she says, shaking her head, staring out across the valley, which is thick with the growth of early summer. I cannot imagine that she is right, for if the river is more full now than usual, certainly it will be higher later in the summer than is normal. With the help of two men Clayton was able to hire, we planted nearly four acres in alfalfa this month and are hopeful of a great harvest.

Your Sister,
Abigail

July 20, 1875

Dear Maggie,

You ask what has become of my drawing and the art work I hoped to take up once we settled in the west. I will tell you. Each morning I wake just before dawn and go outside into the dark desert. The sky is crazy still with stars. They seem to spin and fall in all sorts of ways until the sky is like a large wagon wheel rotating so fast the spokes cannot be distinguished, dirt and clay and stones set flying. Some mornings I stay outside in my wrapper so long among the stars and planets, splashing water on myself, that I see the first streaks of red light to the east as I walk back towards the house. I love best the earliest hours of the day.

When I return to the house I often need to help Clayton get up from the bed if he is stiff upon waking. By now little Margaret is awake, and I sit as long as I can to feed her before hurrying to the stove to fry up hominy cakes or stir porridge. The children dress, and after eating we go into the fields and begin to work the corn or beans or alfalfa. Clayton rides out to check the ditches, and often there are repairs to make. Last month a portion of the bank collapsed and the land flooded. The ditch had to be dried out before it could be dug again.

We have a cow now, which Amy milks before coming to the field. George Michael is already quite adept at feeding the chickens and collecting eggs. I bring the baby to the field and set her on a blanket while Amy and I work.

We stop work for lunch and rest until the sun moves across the sky and the heat lessens. Often in the afternoon, the wind increases, and the heat and sand are driven across the valley in waves. If we do go outside, we must wrap our faces with a cloth. I read to the children and feed the baby; I put on a pot of beans or grain for supper.

Sometimes a neighbor calls on us, or we see burros on the roads, packed with great bundles larger than themselves. There are these few distractions. So you see, by evening when the children are all in bed, I am too tired to get out paper and charcoal, and there is not much light from the oil lamp that hangs over our table.

Doña Romero's prophecy about the dryness of the summer has been borne out, as we have had no rain for three weeks now. I have heard that she is a curandera, someone who can cure sickness, and that she can predict the seasons of drought. She has said that until the moon turns its horns down and lets the water out, we will not have rain. Some evenings when Clayton raises the gate, the ditch is almost dry. He mentioned that this was so while several of them, including Señor López, were repairing the main ditch, and he says there was too little reply made and that he noticed a few mysterious smiles. In the past two weeks we have lost nearly an acre of alfalfa, after all that work of planting and digging the ditches. "Only our second summer, Abigail," Clayton told me, "and I see already how a man could kill for water."

I know you will wonder again, perhaps out loud, why I chose this life, for it is full of difficulty, but in truth I feel it has chosen me. When I walk out into the dry fields and take the crumbling soil in my hands, I feel as if this were the earth I was made of, that I was born to work it. You will say that desires plant themselves inside us, so firmly, so convincingly that we live our lives out of them, believing they are destiny. And perhaps life is a canvas on which our dreams and desires are painted. When the sun sets behind the mountains here, they glitter as if bits of gold had dropped from the sky. So do not be too sorry for me.

Your desert-crazy sister,
Abigail

Chapter 4

February 2, 1876

My Dearest Maggie,

I was filled with grief on reading your letter. To have lost both twins within a few days of each other, and just weeks after they were born—how empty your arms must feel. They left this world as they came into it so little time ago— together. But I know the thought of them with one another is a small comfort, so I will not write to you of it. I am sure that you have been counseled that the Good Shepherd has taken your gentle lambs into His flock. Instead I would tell you that grief is like a mourning cloak that can be re- moved and hung on a high hook but is always with you. Do not turn too quickly to the living. Let sorrow wring your heart until it is emptied. It can be filled again.

If at all possible I will come east next month, as you suggest, and bring the children. I do so want to hold you in my arms.

I am your devoted sister,
Abigail

March 29, 1876

Dear Maggie,

Perhaps we can come at Christmas time. You see, it is difficult to leave a farm—we now have two milk cows and chickens—without considerable planning. I long to be with you now, but I am not certain that Clayton could manage the animals and the planting alone if I were gone. We will plant the four acres in alfalfa and hope to put in a considerable vegetable garden as well.

I am sending a money order with this letter, written to the amount of John's money which Clayton lost to the mines. He has had better luck speculating this past year, and I now sell enough eggs and milk to manage our small household. You must tell Mother not to worry about the living we are able to scrape out anymore, for Aunt Celia has written that Mother does worry, even if she will not write to me of it.

Amy will return in May for the summer. The teachers have written that her progress is exceptional and that she should go on to finish school and attend an academy or a college. She could train in the east for a vocation such as teaching. I cannot tell you what a demand there is out here for teachers.

George Michael plays with a boy who lives nearby. They speak Spanish together, and I cannot understand all that they say. I would like to find him more suitable playmates. Pamela Porter and I meet occasionally to sew or share tea and conversation, but her boys are old enough now to work the ranch with their father. Any schooling they have had she's managed to give them herself with books she brought from Tennessee.

I wish that I could promise to come east by this fall, but after the harvest is finished, the weather will turn quickly and we must prepare wood for the stove. While I do not mean to worry you, for in truth we want for nothing, our life here is a struggle fit to the changes each season brings, and I fear what might happen if we were not prepared.

Now that we have the comforts of a true home, with plenty of bedding, shelves of cookware, and ample provisions, perhaps John will allow you and the children to make the trip westward. I assure you, there are no more wild, scalping Indians. To the contrary, you would find their villages most interesting.

If you can come we will make an outing to one, and you can tell everyone back in Virginia you have met the "savages."

Clayton says that if you come by railroad, we could meet you at the station with the wagon. The trip would not be arduous. We have plans to expand our home, and there would be plenty of space to accommodate you and the children. Until we see one another,

I keep you in my prayers,
Abigail

August 19, 1876

Dear Maggie,

I am writing to you by lantern, as this is the only time I can steal for such things as letters. Our alfalfa cuttings have been more successful than last summer, due in part to an abundance of rain in late June, which has meant water for the ditches all summer. Our neighbor, the old woman Doña Romero, had said it would be so. She watches for signs: the smoke from a newly made fire which settles quickly to the ground, the whirl of ashes in her fireplace, the coyotes' cries.

Last month Clayton and I took her with us to the market place, where we saw her trade for copper bells and the feathers of a song bird. "For use in her incantations," Clayton whispered, smiling. He finds her predictions amusing. But she was right about the water. I cannot tell you what a change it has made not to concern ourselves over each drop spent on dishes or wasted during a washing. There is no animosity between neighbors, only good wishes for a bountiful harvest.

The children are carefree this summer as I have never seen them, Amy nearly dancing through the fields and George running behind her, sometimes charging ahead, with baby Margaret crawling after them through the high grasses, nearly lost in the thick fields of ripening corn. The color, you cannot imagine the color of it all! The deep yellow of the corn, the purple alfalfa, and the fields of dark green bordered by red and white cliffs, all of it covered by the bluest of skies. By next summer, Clayton promises we will have a larger home. Perhaps then you will visit us and see the harvest for yourself. Washed in the brightness of this place,

I am your sister,
Abigail

November 30, 1876

Dear Maggie,

December is nearly upon us, and so I am sending you these few gifts: a ristra made of red peppers, some stones from the mountains, which should delight the children, and a shawl for you, Maggie, one for Irene, and one for Mother, which I have knit of wool spun here in the valley. We wish you the joys of the season.

You asked about the clothing I wear here while working out-of-doors. It is far from what you would call stylish. Last winter I made myself a pair of men's pantaloons of wool, which I wear under a short skirt. It is a practical and somewhat feminine outfit. There are times when I confess I pull on a pair of Clayton's trousers before going out to do the chores. There is seldom anyone who sees me thus outfitted, except for an occasional Mexican on a burro. But yesterday morning as I stood hitching up my pants, having just left the barn with the morning's milking, I saw Señor López sitting on his horse in our drive, his teeth flashing under the brim of his hat. He does not speak much English, and so the joke he might have made about the "Anglo" lady would have been lost to me. I suppose this much was fortunate.

Señor Martínez and his wife, Teresa, took us for a ride last month, and we saw a village which is nearby. The Indians were dancing in the streets, carrying sticks ornamented with feathers and rattles in their hands. They wore white moccasins and leg wrappings. Old men beat drums and sang. Margaret clapped her hands as if it were a parade.

Amy will take the train home soon, and Clayton will meet her with the wagon. We have plans for Christmas Day at the

Deerings' ranch. Their house was completed last summer, and it is quite large, with a wide sitting room and several bedrooms. Clayton has promised that he will add another room to our house by next fall. What a Christmas we will have then!

Your Sister,
Abigail

March 25, 1877

My Dear Maggie,

Patricia was born yesterday morning. She has a blond head of hair and eyes that mirror a desert sky. She is a hearty eater. Margaret has taken to holding my skirt hem all day, and I think she would keep me for herself if she could. I send her out to play in the yard with George and the rabbits they keep as pets.

George has a special love for his little sister. He sets Margaret in a cart and pushes her around the yard. She delights in this and claps her hands, demanding he go faster and faster, until they come charging across the yard, chickens scattering, Margaret screeching. Then she demands to have another "ride," and they start it all again.

Soon it will be planting time, and Clayton is already outside most of the day with the two Mexicans he hired to help with the alfalfa. They will plant an acre or more in peppers also, which we hope to sell at the nearby market.

I regret I could not answer your letters this past winter. When Mother returned the shawl I had made for her, I felt that Virginia was a book I should close and put away on the shelf. All winter, while the snow fell two feet or more, I did not allow myself to think about any of you. Indeed, I feel cut away at times, as if the family of my childhood existed in another lifetime.

But Maggie, there are times when I stop in the middle of planting or cooking or washing the clothes and look out across the valley or up into the mountains, and I long for Stillwater. It is all of a sudden that I miss the streets lined with maples and dogwoods, their pale leaves unfolding, the heavily scented blossoming. You are fortunate, Maggie, that John owns both the store and such a home, the wide columns and those rooms filled with fine furniture, china bowls, and gold-framed portraits. I would I could see it and you for myself again.

The baby is awake. I must return to my duties! I am your happy but tired sister,

Abigail

May 27, 1877

Dearest Maggie,

You write that you are surprised I remember Stillwater after having been gone more than ten years. Has it been as long as that? Would I recognize the streets and the buildings? Have the people changed so much that I would walk the streets a stranger? What I long for most is to hold you in my arms; then I should care not what transformations the rest of the town has undergone.

Patsy is the sweetest baby. I can set her down at any time, for she amuses herself with the simplest things. Yesterday she spent nearly an hour wrapped in her blanket, propped up in a chair, "remarking" over her hands as she waved them in front of herself, curling the little fingers into fists. She delights in watching the other children and sleeps through any noise they make, her features smooth and soft as silk.

It is a blessing to have a baby as easy to care for as she is, for these have been our busiest months, and I cannot imagine how I would help with the planting and accomplish the cooking and cleaning with a colicky infant!

Señora Teresa gave me several fruit tree saplings, which Clayton and the children set into the ground with those she gave us last fall. Then a few days ago she took me to see an old Indian who keeps a substantial herd of sheep. They were well kept, healthy animals, and I have tried to persuade

Clayton to purchase some of them, as I believe I could sell the wool at a profit, but he claims sheep are too much trouble. I suppose they would require more fencing. At any rate, it does not seem I shall get them.

Your Sister,

Abigail

October 7, 1877

Dear Maggie,

We have had another successful harvest. It was a good year again for rain, and we improved one of the ditches. We had so much alfalfa that we hired Mexicans to help with the cutting, and we have an abundance of melons, squash, and every kind of bean. I spend long afternoons shelling out the smooth shiny beans while the children sleep.

Autumn gleams with color here beside the mountains, fields of pumpkins and squash, red oaks and yellow cottonwood. Strings of red peppers are brilliant against the whitewashed adobes. When we took Amy back to school last month, we visited the market, which was crowded with red and green peppers, golden melons, red and blue corn, and the massive Indian jars filled with beans. There were embroidered shawls, strings of prayer beads, moccasins, turquoise, and silver, and sitting in front of a long line of burros was an old man selling ladles made of sheep horns which had been split and hooves that had been turned into rattles. I have heard that these things are kept by witches and used for evil spells, but I do not believe it.

The little ones grow like beans or corn. Someday I will get a picture taken to send to you. Margaret is quick as a jack rabbit and follows George Michael wherever he goes. They run about outside most of the day, even when the wind pushes across the land as if the sky itself had split apart. Patsy is the strongest little baby you ever saw. She crawls everywhere and has thick skin on her knees from crawling over the hot sand.

Amanda Deering has told me that when last she was in Santa Fe she heard of a Dr. Mayfield who had a practice there, and out of curiosity she paid him a visit and found he was the same Thomas Mayfield who had visited Mr. Peerson's ranch. She tried to tell me the details, that he is married, that he travels all over the southwest because of his interest in geology. But I could not make myself hear all of it. After so much time you would think it would not pain me. I wish he had stayed in the east.

Your Sister,
Abigail

April 6, 1878

Dear Maggie,

How quickly the winter has gone, and how many times I thought of you and started to take out my writing box. My only excuses are the usual ones—the animals, the children, the land, and Clayton's trips to the mines, where he is speculating again. We are a busy household, and as you can imagine, our house, to which we added a second room before Patsy was born, is not nearly large enough. We are planning a new house, with wooden floors and a long front porch.

Sister, I am thankful for all the activity. It gives me little time to think on my life and how it has unfolded. You write that you are "content" in your marriage to John, that "married love is naturally burdened by the demands of raising children and earning a living, or perhaps," you said, "love is made stronger by marriage so that it can support these responsibilities." I suppose I expect too much, for when I have the time to reflect, my marriage seems so much without inspiration, and I wonder if Clayton and I were unsuited to one another from the beginning or if we only became distanced, for we are distanced, Maggie, especially these last years since his injury.

Clayton and I have never talked to one another about those months when I thought he had been killed working in the mines. He was dead for me, Maggie, and I had planned the life I would lead without him. The miracle of finding him living was overshadowed by the loss of that life. I know you will understand my meaning. When I heard Thomas Mayfield had married, I wanted to walk out into the desert, into the wind and sand and rock. I would have stood there under the sky until my bones were laid out for the heat and cold, the hard landscape.

I will not write of this again, Maggie, but know it is in my heart.

Your Sister,
Abigail

August 29, 1878

Dearest Maggie,

Thank you for your words of consolation and the pressed irises and roses, which did much to cheer me through the dry heat of these past two months. You have said I am your every concern, but do not worry too much over me. I remember well what Mother said before I came west, that I was too spoiled to live in the fallen world of the south, that I expected more than I would ever get of life. She was right, which means a part of me will always be disappointed. But when I look out across the wide desert, the dark mesa with its long rectangular shape gives me pause and enough peace and wonder that I can smile when Clayton turns to me in the night, I can be glad for the life I have.

This month has been so dry, I fear at times my skin will split apart. There have been curses and evil portents; Doña Romero and Teresa will not say what more is to come. A skull was found in someone's field. In a nearby town, a young woman who had married her closest friend's lover went suddenly mad. And then a week ago we heard that the Deerings' oldest son had been shot while trying to defend their herd.

We harvest the corn and beans, tie up bundles of dark-green alfalfa for sale at the market. There was a man murdered on the road not far from here. Clayton says it was some personal vendetta and that no murderer will come here. But next month while he is away I will keep the shotgun near my hand and one ear listening through the night.

Your Sister,

Abigail

April 2, 1879

Dear Maggie,

All week I have watched the long processions of the Penitents, who walk the road to their church dressed in white trousers, whipping themselves on their back. I have seen their skin redden with welts; it bleeds, and when they become too weak to hit themselves, they beg a friend to do it for them. All afternoon we hear the chains they rattle, the whistles, the loud mournful calls they make with their instruments. Sometimes I think I will go outside and scream at them and not be able to stop. I do not want to hear their suffering. The baby cries, and the children are frightened.

Then today, when I thought I would pack up the children and ride to Pamela Porter's or simply up into the mountains (for you see, Clayton left last week to do some speculating, and so I am alone with all this cacophony), there came, pulled slowly up the road, a large wagon carrying a skeleton. Behind it walked a man who was nearly naked, dragging a wooden cross. I thought of Mary and how I should run out into the road with a cup of water and nearly did, the man was so bent with pain. I have heard they will hang him an hour or more and that he may not live.

"Cannot you believe in Christ without killing some poor fool to prove it?" I asked Teresa. In Virginia they would be arrested for it and should be here, except that we have no laws to prevent barbarity and no one to enforce such laws if they did exist.

It is on days such as these that I feel myself in some foreign land, a place I will never understand. A Methodist preacher and his family and sister have recently moved to the valley to try to convert the Indians. I would like to imagine they will be successful, but five years ago, in a town not far from here, a Presbyterian minister tried to start a church, and the Catholics made a bonfire in the middle of the street of all the hymnals. They claim more missionaries will arrive next week to start a mission school. If it is successful for more than a few months, I will be grateful. George does not read or write with any ease and would rather be in the fields or digging a ditch. His greatest joy is to be on a horse. I have not been able to influence him and therefore welcome any school to the valley where I might send him.

Your Sister,
Abigail

July 28, 1879

My Dear Maggie,

For nearly a month, we have had no rain, and the ditches stand all but dry. The alfalfa is brown, and the fields of beans and corn are filled with brittle, bent stalks. When we open the gate there is nothing but a brown slug of silt. Since the acequia is usually somewhat higher in the morning, Clayton went to the water commissioner, asking that we be given additional hours. He is certain that those upstream from us are using our water, but we have no proof. The water commissioner merely smiled and told Clayton that everyone wants more water these days. "We should pray for the rain."

The night after his trip to the water commissioner, Clayton left the gate up all night, riding out before dawn to close it. Three nights in a row he did this, and we had water again in our fields. On the evening of the fourth night, the water commissioner rode out with a neighbor of ours and Señor López to check the condition of the ditch. While they were here, the water commissioner outlined the fines that apply for misuse of the acequia. Señora Teresa has warned me that we should not resist. She claims Señor López is a powerful man.

We must go to the river for all our water now. I carry what I can and give some water to our vegetable patch, but there is little we can do for the fields of alfalfa. When I look out across them, I feel myself hardening, turning brittle as the stalks of corn, as if the dry wind swept through me, taking with it every drop of moisture.

The children complain of the heat, and I must keep the baby inside much of the day. Yesterday evening when a pack of wild dogs gathered outside the house, I thought they would tear us apart. Clayton shot at them, and finally they scattered, but not until three of them lay dead in the dust. All night we hear the coyotes howl.

I do not think I could get through the day without Amy's help, as she watches the younger children, hauls water, cooks meals, and cleans, all with a cheerful disposition. George is also a help, hauling the water; indeed, for him it is great sport to carry the sloshing buckets. I do believe that most of the time when he spills large quantities of it on himself, it is done on purpose.

Your Sister,
Abigail

November 1, 1879

Dear Maggie,

We had rain, finally, throughout much of late August and September. It was too late to save our fields, but we did harvest a few vegetables. Señor López, who owns the land upstream from us, seems to have lost little of the grain which he grows there. Clayton would not take the corn or beans he sent over in a wagon last month, but while Clayton was away I accepted the few bales of hay, for I do not want to lose our milk cow. Clayton rants against the river and the land; he is certain that we have been cursed. I have tried to convince him that his fears and superstitions are groundless, but at times I am also frightened.

Last week I rode out with Doña Romero to help deliver a baby. The young couple was newly settled from the east and spoke no Spanish, so I had offered to come with Doña Romero. It was late at night and she sat next to me on the wagon seat, when the road was filled suddenly with bats. We buried our faces and covered our heads as their dark wings beat above us. "They've taken the new child's soul," Doña Romero called out, predicting the baby would die at birth.

The baby was born soon after we arrived, alive but black with strangulation, the cord wrapped twice around her neck. I went back yesterday to see if it had lived. She is the prettiest thing, with large blue eyes, her parents' first child and all her mother's delight. I do not see how she can live long, as she is continuously in spasms. The father told me he wants to move to a place more settled as soon as the baby gains its strength. This is a beautiful but isolated place.

Your Sister,
Abigail

January 7, 1880

Dear Maggie,

I hope the package I sent by railroad reached you before Christmas. After such a difficult summer, we were blessed by the holiday. Amy came for two weeks with a friend who goes to the academy, and we had Christmas dinner at the Deerings' ranch, a feast of pheasant, beef, and pork, with all kinds of squash and potatoes. Clayton had luck with his speculations last fall, and while he was in Santa Fe he bought me an easel, material for canvases, and a large box of oil paints. He had made frames and stretched the canvases for me. Everything was wrapped for Christmas.

For many years I thought he saw my desire to paint as something frivolous. So much of our concern was for survival. "I see this cannot wait any longer," he said to me. There are other things we need—a cook stove that is not cracked, a new plow—but he bought me an easel. I have set it up in the far corner of the living room, in front of the window that frames the mesa. The box of paints is open on the table next to it, with the various brushes laid out, so that even if I can spare only a few minutes I can brush color across a canvas.

Mrs. Boswell's poor baby died the day after Christmas. She had grown so weak I did not think she would live to see Christmas, but her mother seemed determined to make her live long enough to shower her with gifts. Mr. Boswell says they will leave for California as soon as the weather is reliable enough for travel.

I have met the new missionary, who will help to start the school. She traveled here alone from the east, riding first in a railway car and then in an old wagon driven by a Mexican and pulled by two burros. She rode this way a full day and most of a night and could not understand a word spoken to her by the driver.

When she at long last arrived at the mission, it was well into the night, and she swears the driver, who must have gotten lost coming over the mountains, had been drinking whiskey from a canteen he kept beside him on the seat. She pushed him aside after they slid off the road for the fourth time and drove herself. It does not sound as if there was much to drive, the burros barely keeping pace with an old Indian woman who walked beside the wagon for several miles and would not accept a ride.

I imagine that when Miss Alden reached the mission and saw how they are supplied—for they have no readers, slates, not even a desk—she wanted to turn back, but she claims she will teach the alphabet by drawing in the dirt with a stick if she must. Already, no matter what the weather, she rides through the valley and even up into the mountains alone on her small, dark horse.

Your Sister,
Abigail

July 1, 1880

Dear Maggie,

Congratulations on Irene's graduation. Does she plan to start work on her teaching certificate next year? I have heard from Aunt Celia all of her accomplishments. And soon Robert will be graduated also. No doubt, John will be glad to have his son working beside him in the store.

This is a busy season, and the canvas I had started to paint last spring sits in the corner of my living room, unfinished. I have marked out the shape of the horizon with the mesa rising up into it and found the right shade of blue for the sky. But these past few months I cannot find the time to paint until it is well into the evening, and by then, of course, it is too dark to look out the window for my inspiration. Clayton says I should put it aside and start another of a still life, perhaps a vase of poppies or roses; we have a trellis of dark-red roses growing near the house.

It is late in the afternoon and raining. Clayton has taken George with him to ride out and check the ditches. Margaret and the baby are sleeping. Recently Señor López, the man we purchased our land from, offered Clayton a mule and a young horse if Clayton will tell him which mines to put his money in. I begged Clayton not to accept. Señor López is a powerful man, and there is no telling what he could do to us if the mines fail. But yesterday evening Clayton rode out to the Lópezes' farm and returned with the mule and the horse. The horse is a mare, silver-gray, marked with white streaks across her back. In the near dark it looked as if Clayton were riding an apparition.

During the last drought Señor López smiled and sent us vegetables from his garden, all the while denying that he kept the gate open and used our share of water. One morning after we had left our gate up through the night, I opened the door and found the hoof of a goat lying in the dirt. Our neighbor Señora Teresa shuddered when she saw it. "It is Señor López's doing," she told me. "There are many who would curse you for him. Let him have the water."

The sky goes on forever and is almost always brilliant and smooth as a piece of satin. Sometimes, in the afternoon, it is a blinding, bare light that makes one empty inside. The people here are the same as the sky, brilliant and warm, distant, terrible. I cannot trust them. As it is, laws do not protect one here. The Boswells left last spring for a more civilized place. Pamela Porter claims we need a sheriff from the east to impose order. "Perhaps," she said last week, "we need an entire militia." Last month the governor resigned, saying there was no way to govern. Anything can happen.

I am watching the light-brown mule from the window I sit at. It is the color of the hills, and there is a patch of evergreen trees not far from the house, the prettiest blue-green against the muddy earth. Perhaps it is them I should paint.

I remain your loving sister,
Abigail

October 12, 1880

Dear Maggie,

Autumn is full of so much color, red, orange, deep purple, yellow, against the bright blue of the sky. I want to paint all of it, and every chance I get I lay out a branch of yellow cottonwood leaves or red peppers and try to match their color. George takes such care of Margaret, and they both love to spend the afternoon out-of-doors. Patsy naps while they play, so that I often take an hour away from the chores of the harvest to do as I please. And an hour seems like such a lot.

Maggie, do not tell anyone, not yet, but I am expecting another child. It should be born sometime early in the spring, perhaps March. I had thought Patsy my last, but I am so looking forward to another. Patsy is our little joy. When I watch her play with a simple rag doll—and she can do this for hours, singing to it or talking with it—I am reminded how easy it is to be happy.

She is Clayton's pet, and he would carry her everywhere if he could. Sometimes he takes her with him when he rides out to the river. She sits in front of him on the saddle, her blond curls gleaming in the sun, a little princess.

The mines Clayton advised Señor López to invest in have not been successful. It was what I warned against, but Clayton claims Señor López understood the risks. We have lost money in them also. So far there has been no hint of retaliation. Teresa and Doña Romero see ill omens everywhere this fall—in the ashes of their fireplaces, in the way the animals behave, in the sky. I try to ignore them. The autumn is so pretty, and we are blessed.

> *Your Sister,*
> *Abigail*

February 2, 1881

Dear Maggie,

We have been struck by influenza. It has taken many in this valley the last few weeks: Señora Teresa's daughter, Señor López's first grandchild. And it has taken my youngest, my last baby. I began to write to you as soon as she was gone, but then I nearly lost Margaret and was, myself, so sick that I delivered early and lost the child I carried.

I am sending a picture we had made of Patricia, our Patsy, in the small wooden coffin. The sickness hollowed out her face, but you can see she had hair the color of sunlight, so much like Josh—oh, both my fair-headed babies. There was no doctor to tend to her. Doña Romero brought *poleo*— an herb to fight fever—and a specially made oil. She stayed the night, counting her beads. Nothing comforts me.

Oh, Maggie, last night I walked out onto the earth and looked into the sky. I felt her close to me, touching the hem of my wrapper. When I closed my eyes I felt Josh there too, twisting his fingers in my hair, the way he did as I carried him a long way from home. The stars slid across night's bowl, a wild sprinkling of light. The night of Patsy's death, I thought Clayton would go mad, but soon he had to nurse me and Margaret; he could not afford the time to grieve. At his insistence, we buried Patsy and the infant in a small patch of ground that looks down on the river, where she loved to ride sitting in front of Clayton on his horse.

Life is blown away quick—not more than three weeks ago I watched Patsy playing on the rug with her toys and thought how perfect each gleaming hair on her head, how sweet each busy finger. In mourning, I am your sister.

Abigail

May 20, 1881

Dear Maggie,

I have not been able to "get free" of all this sadness, as you suggest I do in your letter. I do not want to plant a garden or cook a meal or even paint. I do not care if the alfalfa is planted on time. Pamela Porter has asked me to speak with the new minister, and I suppose I shall. But I do not care even to hear a friend's advice.

The desert is strung with flowers: blossoming cacti, the red and orange Indian paintbrush, and the prairie torch, whose flowers line its stalk like small white bells. Yesterday Clayton and I rode up into the mountains through the brightly colored blossoming. The prickly pear were covered with their large, fleshy flowers, and for the first time I hated them for how sensuous, how prolific, how incredibly beautiful they were. It is the same with Margaret. I cannot bear to watch her play or feel her small, plump hand on my arm. I cannot help it that I turn away.

We have started work on our house, a ranch house with a pitched roof and a long, deep porch. Last night while Clayton and I worked in the fields, the sun streaked across the sky until the mountains beneath it turned the many shades of purple. It saddened me.

Abigail

Karen Osborn

March 3, 1882

Dear Maggie,

Amy is a young lady now. How quickly it happens! Irene, Amy, Robert—can it be they are grown? She finished her schooling this past winter and is determined to complete her teaching certificate. To do this, she wants to return east. It is my hope that she might stay with you and attend the teachers' college with Irene. When she gets her certification, she will return to New Mexico to teach. After all the years of separation, Maggie. If possible, I will bring Amy east myself so that we can see one another again.

Our house has five large rooms, and even in the winter they are thick with light. I have planted climbing roses and grapes along one end of the wide porch. This year George has attended the nearby mission school begun by Miss Alden and the reverend and his sister. The school is now furnished with an organ, maps, a blackboard, readers, slates, and even pens and ink. Several white children from the surrounding homesteads attend, but the majority of the students are the Indian children whom the missionaries have come to convert. The older Indian girls bring babies with them, as it is their job to care for their younger siblings. If George had his way, he would not attend school at all, for already he seems sure that he wants to spend his life working on a ranch. It is not a life I would have chosen for him. The ranchers are a rough bunch. Their lives grow out of the desert sand and rock and clay. You can hardly imagine anything like them back in Virginia.

Clayton and I and the children spend much of our time simply keeping the farm in operation, caring for the animals, planting and harvesting. When Clayton is gone speculating, I am here alone with the children. Last month while he was away, we had a snowstorm, and so it was three weeks before he was able to come home. Señora Teresa sent her son to see if we had fuel and food, but other than this we saw no one.

George, who was home from the mission school, and Margaret were a great help feeding the animals, but they long to spend all their time outside in the fields or riding through the red hills and grew quite bored with sitting around the stove. During the storm, they quarreled so often I nearly sent them out into the drifting snow.

The pleasure of another lady's company is a rare treasure. Pamela Porter and I have become the best of friends, but we seldom see one another because of the distance between our lands. When we are able to visit, we eagerly trade issues of *Godey's* and discuss the fashions and all that has transpired in our lives. The new Methodist minister preaches a sermon every other Sunday, and we enjoy the service and seeing the other families. A picnic is sometimes held, and after days, sometimes weeks, of speaking mostly Spanish with our neighbors, we enjoy both the food and the conversation.

Maggie, I do not understand the course my life has followed. Often it seems a curse comes with a blessing. I have fallen in love again, and with my own husband. After we buried Patsy, for months I could not bear to see him, but then at the end of last year's summer I sat in the garden, which Clayton had filled with flowers and cacti and beautifully shaped rocks before even the house was finished. There were purple verbena and roses. As I sat in the quiet fire of that blossoming, my life one thin thread, quick and full of gleaming, there was a movement behind me, slight as a breeze sifting through my hair. Then Clayton's hand was on my shoulder.

"I feel as if we're all here," I said to him. "In this garden. Patsy and Josh and the baby I would have had, all of us, a family. I feel as if we're whole here, even you."

Clayton nodded. "It's a wondrous place, Abigail," he told me. "A heaven on earth. I'm sorry for what we lost, but not sorry we came."

Something has changed, and a new tenderness exists between us. There is, it seems, so much for us to share: rides up to the mesa, where the river falls through the trees like a length of turquoise sky and the colors of the land (orange, red, yellow, green, brown) overlay one another in endless patterns below. The sky is so close it fills our lives with light, harsh yet brilliant. It is as if we are spun together, Clayton and I, in a web of glittering sky. At night the stars and planets turn, an explosive wheel above us, until sometimes, walking with Clayton through the garden or out into the yard, I am dizzy with light.

When Fernando, who does occasional chores for us, came yesterday with a stack of wood, he told a story about the formation of the heavens, in which the stars were kernels of corn that had spilled from a basket one of the gods carried on his head. "And now still they feed us," he said.

Clayton nodded when Fernando finished. "They feed us."

Last fall Clayton helped me order a selection of art supplies—paints, charcoal, paper, and more canvases. In the evening when the weather allows, I sit in the garden drawing or painting. I have completed a few landscapes with the mesa in the background. Clayton claims one of these as his favorite.

I want to paint the priests in their wide hats and vestments on their way to mass, the farmers in their cornfields, the little Indian children at the mission school, the ranchers on horseback, their faces thick with red dust. And I want to paint the sky. Perhaps I will send you these paintings so that you can know my life for yourself.

I am your sister,
Abigail

Chapter 5

May 4, 1882

Dear Maggie,

Amy will take the train east, arriving at the station in Richmond on the fifteenth day of August. I am sending you the schedule of her departure and arrival, and while we have been told that the trains are punctual, I cannot guarantee it. Let me know of your plans for meeting her, so that I can give her accurate instructions. She is most excited about the trip and filled with anticipation over the pleasure of meeting, after so many years, her "eastern family."

Maggie, the fare for the trip was more than I had anticipated, and as much as I long to accompany her, my trip east will have to wait. With the combined costs of our new house and Amy's schooling (despite the generous scholarship, there are a number of costs), we have little to spare. I am only grateful there is enough to send Amy and that she will receive the best possible of educations. If not for the war, both you and I would perhaps have been educated there. What a different world it would have been.

I have purchased cotton broadcloth, linen, and several yards of wool with which to outfit her. We spent several evenings last week bent over my issues of *Godey's,* trying to determine the latest styles. Amy chose a suit with drapery in the back, and I will make her a white blouse and a dark wool skirt. I am enclosing a sketch of the suit so that you can tell me whether or not it is the fashion there. Amy does want to dress in style, and I fear we are behind.

Your Sister,
Abigail

July 10, 1882

Dear Maggie,

Amy has instructions to meet you at the railroad station on August fifteenth at four-thirty in the afternoon. She will be wearing a blue dress and carrying a valise inscribed with her initials. I have told her to notify us of her arrival at once by telegram. Clayton and I will be quite anxious for her.

We have had no rain for six weeks now; the ditches are low. Clayton is sure we will get no more cuttings of alfalfa, as the fields are brown and nearly barren. There was a new family from Alabama that bought land a few miles south of here and built a house this past spring. They stopped by yesterday afternoon and announced they are moving farther west to California. "With no rain, it is like living on a desert," they told me. "How do you survive?" They had come here as we did, unaware of the peculiar laws that govern water rights and taking for granted that the most precious of resources would always be available.

How do I survive, Maggie? It seems we will never know for certain how much of our water our neighbors use during a drought, but the mere suspicion is enough to cause bad will. And now another family come from the east that will not stay. Except for each other, George and Margaret have only the Spanish-speaking children as playmates. They catch horned toads and snakes and dig in the clay. I hear them singing Spanish songs, and I cannot understand the words. In the evenings they repeat the tales they have heard of animals and treasures, of a boy who was turned into a wolf, of phantom horse riders.

Virginia feels as far away as another continent. But

perhaps, through Amy, we two can be reunited. I shall sigh with relief as soon as I get word that she is in your hands.

Your Sister,

Abigail

August 18, 1882

Dear Maggie,

The telegram has arrived, and oh that I were there with you also! I do long for the happy reunion we would make. I cannot convey the depth of my concern after leaving Amy in the railroad car. We pray that she is content while staying with you and that her progress is worthy of the scholarship she has received. Take care of her for me.

Your Sister,

Abigail

December 12, 1882

Dear Maggie,

Amy writes that she will spend a pleasant holiday in your home. I thank you for welcoming her. She writes also of her frequent visits with Mother, who, she tells us, is gracious in every way and has bought her another dress, a silk blouse, and a woolen skirt, and made presents to her of hair ribbons and laces. I had not thought that a young woman attending school would need such ornaments, but Amy writes that fashion is more extravagant in the east. I know you will understand my meaning when I tell you that I am grateful for Mother's attentions but do not want my daughter moved in any way against me.

I have sent a few small things along with Amy's package for your Christmas. Surely, it will be a joyful one.

Your Sister,
Abigail

April 2, 1883

Dear Maggie,

Amy writes that she is content to remain in Stillwater for the summer, continuing her studies. My thanks to you for extending her such a welcome and encouraging her in her work. Indeed, I am blessed to have a family that devotes itself to my child after I have been away these many years. I miss her more than I can write, and have pictured her here during the summer months, painting or sewing with me in the garden, playing with the children, and riding out along the river or to the mesa. But we are just now short of funds (last summer was so dry), and it is best that we hold on to the money that would pay for her ticket.

Nine years we have lived in this valley, and still I do not understand the patterns of dryness and rain. Perhaps there is no discernible pattern, only the certainty that one will lead to the other. We have had little rain all year, each day the sky stretching wide and blue across the valley and over the mountains, the color of heaven. Maggie, it is so beautiful, I cannot curse it as Clayton does at times.

The children are well. Margaret cannot be separated from her brother. She rides a little dappled pony, and George rides his horse. They go everywhere, up and down the valley, along the river, into the mountains. When they are gone long hours in the afternoon, I worry some mishap has befallen them, but they always return safely in time to do their chores, and I think that it must be good to be able to roam under the wide sky. Such freedom is usually reserved for boys. I cannot imagine Margaret without it.

It seems this past year we have all been unusually healthy. Doña Romero says it is the drought, a blessing inside a curse, but I believe one's constitution is strengthened by one's hardships.

Your Sister,
Abigail

August 7, 1883

Dear Maggie,

At last it has rained, torrents all through the past two weeks, breaking over us each afternoon and often throughout the night. It comes too late for the alfalfa, but we will have a small field of beans, our vegetables, and the little corn we managed to irrigate. This has been the longest drought we have had since coming to the southwest. Throughout the winter, spring, and early summer, farmers in the valley slaughtered their animals as there was nothing left to feed them. Everywhere one went, one could see dead pigs, goats, and chickens. "I cannot stand to see any more death," I told Clayton last spring when we rode past our neighbors and saw their milk cow lying in the yard, its throat cut. Two days later Clayton himself went out and shot the goat Margaret had made a pet of.

When the first rain fell, I was in the house preparing the week's bread for the oven. Clayton and George had ridden out to look with despair on the dried-up ditches, and I had sent Margaret to find the chickens that had disappeared. As I shaped the loaves, I looked outside and saw the darkening of the sky. I told myself that after all these months, it was merely another mirage. And so I did not step out into the yard until the storm was nearly upon us, racing up the valley with the whirling of dark clouds and the explosion of thunder. As I ran through the yard, I heard Clayton and George in the barn, trying to quiet the horses. "Where is Margaret?" I called out, but I could not hear the answer through the wind.

She rode into the barn shortly before the rain began. I saw her from the house in a flash of lightning, bent over the pony's neck, white as an apparition. She had ridden out towards the mountains to watch the approach of the storm, she told us later, and it is a wonder she survived. Had she not been so sure in the saddle, I fear we would have lost her.

Maggie, she is a good girl, really, and spends hours in the fields and helping us with the animals, but she will not sit still long enough to learn to read or embroider. When she is not with George, she is alone, running through the yard or fields or out into the orchard. She begs me to let her take her pony and ride along the river or up towards the mesa, and sometimes I allow it, Maggie, even though she is young. It seems to me she has few amusements. Clayton tells me that given time she will grow into a lady. I only hope he is right and that the desert has not bewitched her.

Yours,
Abigail

September 28, 1883

Dear Maggie,

This has been the strangest of seasons. With the rain has come a late flowering throughout the valley and even out into the deserts and mountains. I cannot adequately describe it, but after so many dry months, the air has thickened with the various fragrances. My good neighbor Señora Teresa Martínez calls it a time of miracles. Another neighbor of ours was working in his fields just after an evening rain, when he was startled by voices above him. He looked into the sky and saw a magnificent balloon.

As he watched, a woman threw an armful of roses, which drifted downward. When the balloon disappeared, he assumed it had been an apparition, but the scent of roses was everywhere, and in his hair he found a soft red petal.

The rain seems to make everything possible. Last Sunday Clayton and I and the children rode out for Reverend Brown's service at the church. The Porters were there, the Sloaners, a new family I had not met, Miss Alden, and several others. It seemed to have been so long since I had seen any of them. What a reunion we had, singing hymns together and later drinking tea, which Miss Alden had brought. Our ride home was filled with the strange beauty of the wildflowers and blossoming cacti. Even a few of the trees, confused by the long drought and sudden flood, had burst into white blossoms. "An unusual heaven," Clayton commented, and I had to agree.

I have made arrangements to send both Margaret and George to the mission school this year. If Margaret remains at home another year, I feel she will turn completely to the wild. She follows George and Ramon, Señora Teresa's son, up towards the mountains, herding goats and sheep. I cannot keep her indoors. The only way I have been able to convince her to attend school is to tell her she will be able to travel to and from school riding on her pony with her brother.

The Catholic priests persist in their attempts to destroy the mission school. They clearly are responsible for a number of Indian children being pulled out of the school and have tried, unsuccessfully, to have the school's land taken away. The school survives mainly due to personal donations from local families and a few of the churches in the east. If not for the Catholics, we would have public schools in New Mexico and not an embarrassingly high number of illiterate, well over half the population. I have heard that many of the mining towns now have public schools. But there are so many Catholics in the valley, I do not think we will see such progress here.

Amy writes that she is doing well in her studies. Please send word at once if she wants for anything. She is young to be so far from her parents, and sometimes, despite the reassurance of your loving care, I become anxious for her.

Your Grateful Sister,

Abigail

December 18, 1883

Dear Maggie,

Amy writes that she grows despondent with the approach of the holiday season. I have no doubt the parties she wrote she would attend will create a more cheerful attitude, but I am anxious for her. Please, Maggie, give her a mother's love and comfort for me. I miss her more than I can express.

I understand that Mother has bought her a dress for the holiday celebrations. Amy says it is made of deep-green velvet, with satin trim and rows of white pearly buttons, and that it is long-waisted, cut in the latest fashion. I do not know of anything that I can make to equal such a dress. All this month I have spent crocheting a lace bed spread and pillow shams. If I can finish them by next week, I will mail them for Amy's Christmas. I have prepared a package for you also, Sister, and will send them together by railroad.

Yours,

Abigail

March 1, 1884

Dear Maggie,

The first of March, and still snow covers the ground like lit crystal under the sun, a blinding slick whiteness covered with a thin sheen of ice. Clayton tried to persuade me to ride out to the mesa with him this afternoon, when the hard crust had softened with a watery beauty, but I convinced him to take George and Margaret, as I am feeling poorly. Perhaps I have only been cold for too long and must climb into my bed until this season passes.

Perhaps I will take out my paints and commit one of my sketches to the canvas. Last week I finished a portrait of Pamela Porter, and she seemed pleased with the effect. Oh, Maggie, it is on afternoons such as these that I miss my Amy most, and if I dwell on her too much, all that I've lost through the years takes form and I cannot be convinced of this life's purpose.

But do not worry yourself. I will take out my paints and stroke the canvas with my brush, bringing back all color and brightness into my world.

I am your sister,
Abigail

May 26, 1884

Dear Maggie,

I am sending a money order for Amy's train ticket so that she may come home this summer. If you would, please cash it for her. I thank you, again, for all you have done. Her letters are filled with the kindnesses you have given. I am truly grateful. We will welcome Irene if she still wishes to make the train trip west with Amy. I know they have grown fond of one another, but that is not surprising—they are our daughters!

This has been a spring of flowering, one spring like this only every fifty or sixty years, our Spanish neighbors tell me. Everything has blossomed at once, so that the desert is pink, blue, and yellow, like a colored map. Yesterday Clayton and I rode up towards the mesa. Even the rock was striped with colors, bands of gold and red and pink. "Paint it, Abigail," was all Clayton could say. "Paint it just the way the colors lie now."

The purple verbena covers the garden like a carpet, and the apple trees which Clayton planted in the orchard are heavy with blossoming. I would that I could spend all day in it.

Shortly after sunrise, I bake biscuits and fry eggs for Clayton, George, and the two Mexicans that help with the planting. Margaret eats the hominy we make from our corn, cooked with eggs. After breakfast, when the men go to the fields, George goes with them. He is as tall as I am and would be on a horse all day if he could. When the house is in order, I send Margaret to the fields with water, if she has not already gone to ride along the ditches with her brother or help with the planting. There are also the cows to be milked and the chickens which must be fed. It is after dinner, when the sun touches the mountain tops, before I can sit in my garden.

We will hope to see both girls by the end of June. We do so want to meet Irene. I know we do not have as many social occasions, which you write that they so enjoy, but I am sure they will be so busy exploring this strange and various country that they will not have time to wish for parties to attend!

Your Loving Sister,
Abigail

July 28, 1884

Dear Maggie,

It has been a joy for us to have the two young ladies in our house. The singing and laughter that have filled the rooms make me feel a girl again. Each evening after supper we sit in the garden under the shade of the cottonwoods and read poetry aloud. In the afternoons they often paint or draw.

And they have taught Margaret her arithmetic. I am sure both of them will make admirable teachers. You should know that Irene was offered a post not more than fifteen miles from here. If she takes it, she and Amy will be headmistresses at neighboring schools!

While we have enjoyed Irene immensely, and of course she is welcome in our home at any time, you may think it wise to shorten this visit. Being here is a little like visiting another country, and young people often romanticize what is new and undiscovered to them.

A few weeks ago there was a Fourth of July barbecue held at the Deerings' ranch. Amy and Irene were quite excited, as the barbecue is a big affair held each year, which lasts the day and into the evening, with all kinds of food and games, music and dancing. The six of us rode out to the Deerings' the morning of the Fourth. Oh, you should have seen the decorations! Long tables were covered with bright table cloths on which platters of steaks with every kind of vegetable and breads had been set. Streamers made of red, white, and blue cloth hung from long poles stuck into the ground. And the people were dressed so that they could be called decorations too. Irene and Amy both had tucked tiny flags into their hats and wore their blue suits with the long wide skirts.

There was much eating and gossiping that afternoon. It had been a year or more since I had seen many of these neighbors, and I was lost in a flurry of greetings and news and reminiscences. Amy, Irene, and George joined the young people. The Deerings raise a large herd of cattle, and so there were a number of young cowboys in their wide-brimmed hats prancing around on horses and showing off their abilities with a rope.

I overheard Amy try to pull her cousin away from a ring they had created to ride in. "They only want to create a spectacle," she said. But Irene did not want to leave the crowd which had gathered around them. It is difficult not to watch them; they are so agile, so full of quick grace.

Later when I looked up from my conversation with Mrs. Coleman, whose daughter had just gotten married the month before, I saw how the sun had sunk and that they were getting ready to light the fireworks display. I found Amy and asked where Irene had gone. It took me several minutes to get the truth from her, that Irene and a young ranch hand had taken two of the horses and gone riding. I immediately spoke with the Deerings and was assured that the ranch hand was a responsible young man, the son of a friend of Mr. Deering's who had settled in Utah.

By the time they returned, Irene breathless from the ride, the fireworks had ended. Later that night I explained to her that going riding with a young man, especially a young cowboy, out here is different than going out walking with a young man in Stillwater. In her mind I am sure it was no more than a friendly ride through the desert, but I suspected the boy had more in mind, as I heard him ask if he could ride out to visit her later in the week.

Several times now, despite the distance between our land and the Deerings' ranch, he has called on Irene. They go out riding is all that she will tell us, and I do not doubt her word but fear for her reputation. Mr. Deering has told Clayton the young man would marry Irene if it comes to this, but I am not sure you would want a young cowboy for a son-in-law.

If you think it wise we can send Irene back to Virginia a week or two early. I am quite sure Amy would agree to accompany her so that she would not have to travel alone. Once Irene is back in Virginia, I know she will forget this ranch hand, as she is a sensible young lady.

I am your devoted sister,
Abigail

August 20, 1884

Dear Maggie,

I am dismayed by your accusations that it was my influence, or lack of influence, that caused Irene's indiscretions. Irene is not a child anymore, and surely she is accountable for her own mistakes. I assure you, living in the west has not caused me to "loosen" my values so much that I no longer can "tell what is right from what is wrong." When you comment that my notions about love lack the maturity of a woman my age, I wonder that you could be so "mature." I would hope that I am never so old.

Maggie, you have been my one true confidante. How can you judge my life so harshly? Did you use my confessions to strengthen the blame which you falsely laid on me? I can picture you in Virginia attending socials and helping out at the church and at John's store, and in the house that was given to you by John's parents with its wide and gracious porch, under the shade of the magnolias and oaks, sitting in judgment on my life when you know how I have had to struggle to shape it myself, the best that I could.

I have written to Amy that she is to return home in April upon completion of her certificate. The school east of North Valverde is expecting her to begin the following fall, and she will need a good part of the summer to prepare her classroom and her lessons. In the event that she is no longer welcome at your home, I have sent her money enough to board elsewhere while she finishes her studies. I shall write to Aunt Celia. Perhaps she will assist Amy in finding a suitable place.

Your Sister,
Abigail

October 13, 1884

Dear Maggie,

Amy has written that she is "most welcome" in your home and plans to stay with you through the spring while she completes her certificate. I am grateful that your judgments of me do not extend to Amy. I know she is looking forward to completing her studies so that she may return to the west.

She writes that Irene's new suitor is the son of Mr. Clyde Baker. I remember Mother's wish that one of us might marry "a Baker boy." It is a good family. I am happy for you.

It has been two months now since I sent you a letter, and I had thought you would write back to me. Aunt Celia has not written since the spring. Have you divulged any of your doubts about my lack of judgment or morality? I pray that you have not betrayed my confidences. Amy has said that Mother is not well. Please write to me if she is declining. I shall come east at once despite your ill feelings towards me. I wish very much to make a reconciliation with her.

Your Sister,
Abigail

January 14, 1885

Dear Maggie,

You write that if I were truly in mourning, I would come east for Mother's funeral and pay my respects. You know nothing of the depths of my grief and remorse. If I had not heard from Amy that Mother had taken to her bed, I would have known nothing, so little care did you take to keep me informed. Had you written to me truly as a sister should, I would have come at once to attend her. Instead you expect me to come now, after there is no hope of reconciliation. You expect me to come and sit at her funeral when everyone in the church will know that she had refused my letters.

I cannot believe you when you say that you had not expected an end and that her illness was sudden. Did she not take to her bed last September? And as for your love for me, I feel these are words at best, empty of any substance. I shall let Amy take my part at the funeral. I shall not return east.

Abigail

June 5, 1885

Dear Maggie,

It has been five months since Mother's death. Until last week, I thought I would not write to you again, for I do not think I will ever forget that you took from me any chance that Mother would welcome me back into her keeping before her death. But now I see that there is more betrayal that binds us. Even now that Mother is no longer alive, you have the ability to alter the course my life runs.

Amy's latest letter states that she has refused the teaching post offered to her in New Mexico and that she has a suitor who will write to Clayton asking her hand in marriage. Now you stand between me and my daughter as you stood for so long between me and Mother. She writes that his name is Everett Turner and explains that he is from a good family, as if I did not know the name, as if Sally, the closest friend of my girlhood, were not the boy's aunt.

Stillwater appears in her letters as if some magical kingdom, with its paved streets and buggies, the men in coats and hats and ladies in silk or taffeta basques, with stiff petticoats and ruffles, their hair tied with ribbons. Has she shown you the bustle I once taught her to make by folding a thick towel over a string? I suppose you had a long laugh at our simple poverty. Now Amy tells me she wears only suits and dresses that are in fashion.

I am an outsider to this world where one can buy soft, narrow-toed shoes and a new hat for every season. I did not know that Japanese parasols are carried in the sun or that the Inmans hold a ball each spring. Do the mimosa trees still drape over the sidewalks on Chelsea Avenue, and do the ladies gather on the porches along Vine Street to hear the latest gossip? I cannot imagine a Stillwater that is any different than the one I left eighteen years ago.

Maggie, know that it is not the young man himself that I object to, only that I have lost too much in this world already. I cannot face the loss of my own dear Amy, and it will be a loss if she marries this boy, for I feel sure they will settle near his home.

The wide sky that stretches over our ranch seems too full of light this summer, fragile and empty. Clayton and George have gone to check on a mine that Clayton plans to invest in. I have sent Margaret to play at a neighbor's house, for she needs company her own age, even if they do speak Spanish. If Amy were here, I would ride with her to a grove of piñon trees that grows along the base of the mountains. They are so pretty against the sandy hills.

I remain your sister,
Abigail

Chapter 6

September 29, 1885

Dear Maggie,

Clayton has given his consent so that Amy and Everett Turner may wed. It went against him to do so. But she would only resent our interference, and we will not force her to live in New Mexico. Amy writes that the wedding will take place this winter in the Turners' home. Clayton refuses to attend, insisting she should be married out here. Now that his oldest brother has moved to Denver, he has no family ties left in Virginia and will not leave the ranch for the two or three weeks we would need to make the trip.

I will plan to take the train east with Margaret. Amy

is my oldest and dearest daughter, and as you say, I could not bear to miss her wedding. I will look forward to seeing you also, Maggie, despite our quarrels. When we were young, each thought I had could have easily been yours. I knew all of you—your quick, fluttering gestures, the sadness that stayed in your eyes for months after we heard about Father's death, and the brightness that came into your voice the summer you met John. I hope you are not right in saying we no longer know one another. But perhaps time and distance, wide as the sky, have lain down between us.

Your Sister,
Abigail

December 7, 1885

Dear Maggie,

George Michael has disappeared. Last week he asked Clayton to let him ride twenty miles north to a ranch and help move cattle. George was supposed to be in school, and the weather is unpredictable this time of year. Clayton told him he could not make the trip. All last summer George begged us to let him ride out to the Deerings' ranch and help out, but there were not many days Clayton could spare him. He has always been a mindful boy but recently talked

163

of nothing but ranching and being a cowhand, so there is no telling what he will do.

It is more than a week he has been gone. Margaret is despondent, and I fear that if not for the cold she would try to follow him. Clayton rode up north, where the rancher, a Mr. Robertson, told him that some of the boys went farther north towards Colorado, to get on with a bigger ranch. We fear that George went with them. Clayton blames himself for allowing George to help with cow herding last summer, but had he not allowed it, I doubt he could have prevented George from going. Out here the boys are wild as wolves or coyotes, and nobody can do a thing with them.

I have written to Amy saying I will plan to come in January to help with all the preparations. I pray George is returned to us safely by then. We had several inches of snow last night. By morning the sun came out and the sky turned a hard, brittle blue. Now, in the late afternoon, there is a thin sheen across the snow where the sky melted it, then froze it to a blue ice. The whole world has turned blue. When there is snow here, there is more of it north, where George Michael must have ridden.

Your Sister,
Abigail

January 25, 1886

Dear Maggie,

You must know how much I wanted to board the train last week, how much I want to be there with my daughter, helping to prepare for the wedding. Aunt Celia writes that all of you are pleased with the union Amy will make and that I must come soon, for my delay gives the appearance that I still harbor some resentment. Maggie, please convince Aunt Celia of my sincere desire to be in attendance. As I have written to both Amy and Aunt Celia, I will come as soon as I can, but I am afraid to leave with George gone and Clayton in a heated fury over it.

Indeed, Clayton would have ridden out before now to look for our boy, except that the weather has been so fierce. Snowstorm has followed snowstorm for more than a month now, and if there is not some respite soon, we will be hip or waist deep. It is with some difficulty that we manage simple tasks such as feeding the animals, and Margaret has not attended school since Christmas. We have heard that the trains are still running with some regularity, but the trip will certainly be more difficult to make in this weather.

Earlier this month I wrote to Amy asking if she could delay the wedding until spring, but as she pointed out, that time of year is one of the busiest for us, and all of the invitations have been sent. I have finished sewing Margaret's dress, a green plaid silk, long-waisted, with two rows of pearl buttons. Amy insists that I wait and buy my own dress when I reach Virginia, but I will alter my blue velvet to bring in the event that I reach Stillwater with no time to spare before the wedding. I can only hope that conditions will change so that I can make the trip, however hasty it might be. But, Maggie, if I cannot, give what I have enclosed, a mother's words, to Amy the morning of the wedding.

Your Sister,
Abigail

January 1886

My Dear Daughter,

    Here are the pressed flowers I had thought to bring you, a bit of desert to scent your clothes, a wedding sachet of verbena, yellow roses, and the petals from a flowering cactus. Marriage is not something that is always easy, year after year. But you can make of your life what you will have of it; know that, dearest Amy, for I have always wished for you the best of life.

    I send this letter and the flowers in your Aunt's care that in the event I cannot be there, she may give them to you the morning of your wedding. Know that like the desert scent, I am with you. I wish that I were not held here so tightly.

I know that you will be the loveliest of brides. Oh! that I could see you in your dress, touch for myself the lace of your veil, brush out your fine hair, hold you, Daughter, in my arms those moments before you are given away to a life of your own making. I am with you, Amy; I am there as you walk into the church, as you say your vows to Everett, like the color and scent of these flowers.

I send you my love,
Your Mother

February 25, 1886

Dear Maggie,

Amy writes that the wedding was beautiful despite the terrible cold and that all the ladies wore white or a pale pink so that the room looked like winter itself had come indoors. You must know how I envy you playing my part, but I am grateful Amy was not left there alone to be a bride. This will be one of my deepest regrets, to have missed my daughter's wedding. I do not think that I shall ever forget it.

We still have no word from George. There are days when Margaret refuses to go to school and despite the ice and cold takes a horse and rides out into the desert. Clayton has ridden north and returned without news. He thinks George is somewhere waiting out the winter and will come back home in the spring. Even as a boy, George always took care of himself, and I must hope he is doing that now.

I have put the pieces of material Amy sent that were from her dress and veil in a frame.

I remain your sister,
Abigail

April 2, 1886

Dear Maggie,

Amy has written she and Everett are nicely settled in the house Everett's parents provided for them and that Everett has begun to practice law and she is teaching at the academy. I sent her a set of dishes made in Mexico to remind her of the land she grew up on, and the silver spoons passed down from Grandmother. I know that she is content to be surrounded by books at the academy and busily attending dinners and the orchestra and church functions with her husband.

Our lives here continue to rotate with the seasons. As soon as the ground dries enough to work the soil, we will put in our crops. Clayton has hired four or five Mexicans to help with the planting, for we have decided to add more acres of both corn and alfalfa. Several ditches will need to be dug, along with the planting. The snow that fell this winter has seeped down into the earth, so that the soil is as wet as I have ever seen it. We are hopeful of a good harvest.

Margaret is becoming as wild as George. There is not a thing I can do with her, or the teacher either. We send her to school each morning on a gentle spotted mare, but yesterday the teacher told us Margaret has not been to school in a week's time. When we asked her where she had been, she only stared out the window as if she could not hear us. Pamela Porter tells me that some of the young people gather in front of the store beside the mission school, hoping for excitement. But Clayton thinks she is all the time out riding through the valley and the desert. I am afraid for her.

Yesterday morning Clayton rode in to deliver her to the teacher. Miss Alden has suggested that she board there until the end of the term. I have tried to teach her fine embroidery and quilting, but she has no patience if the thread should break or get a knot. She is not like Amy and refuses to learn her lessons, staring out of the window or making some excuse so that she can leave her work. I do not know what will become of her.

Your Sister,
Abigail

August 30, 1886

Dear Maggie,

This summer has been spent so quickly. Clayton's brother and his family were here for a visit in early May. Clayton's nephew, Steven, had recently finished university studies in geology and was most interested in the southwest landscape. To oblige him, all of us made a five-day camping trip to the northwest corner of the territory. We came across some unusual red sandstone formations and caves that had been built into the walls of the cliffs. Steven stayed behind to work with an expedition that has begun to uncover geological findings.

I believe Clayton and I enjoyed the trip as much as his nephew. We took numerous hikes up along the red cliffs where the earth falls away into the sky. Clayton and his brother fished in the streams. It was like being on holiday.

As you know, the entire month of June, Amy and Everett were here. Everett seems the ideal husband for Amy, knowledgeable, thoughtful, kind. They spent most of their time out-of-doors, walking through the orchard or down to the river. The cacti were still flowering, and Everett had never seen anything like it. I took the young couple up and down the valley so all of our neighbors could greet them. Señora Teresa gave Amy a shawl painted with flowers and birds. There were piles of linens and table settings and finely wrought candlestick holders. Pamela Porter had made a quilt. When they left on the train, we had to have everything boxed for shipment; there was so little of it that could be squeezed into their luggage.

We have heard, finally, from George. He is in Colorado, working on a ranch, and plans to herd cattle south for wintering. There was nothing but to give him our blessing; still, I will think of him often. He is just a boy, and it is a man's work there on the open land. I wish that he would return and perhaps enter some sort of college, but he has never gleaned much from books. Even when he was a young child I never saw him happy except when he was outside. Perhaps he is meant to work that way, his feet on the solid ground, breathing the sky itself.

We ladies in the valley have formed a lively sewing circle, which meets this evening at Pamela Porter's house. The Reverend's wife and his sister attend, and a Mrs. Townsend and Mrs. Sloaner as well. The local gossip is discussed over the quilts. All of the recent talk is over whether or not Mr. Berns will return to his wife and small child. When he brought his wife west to live on the land he had purchased, she planned to have a millinery, the first and finest shop of its kind in this part of the country. She soon saw what a disaster such an undertaking would be here and resigned herself to raising children and farming a piece of land that is so far from the river it is really a piece of desert.

Three weeks ago he disappeared, gone I suppose to some mining town in Colorado or perhaps California. He is a gambler and cannot live in a place that has no saloons. Mrs. Sloaner claims his young wife is left with a ten-month-old baby and a room full of fabrics and ribbons and feathers and hats. We have invited her to our meetings, but she has yet to attend one.

I have tried to convince Margaret to accompany me to the sewing circle, but she is not one to sit quietly with a needle and thread or a book. All day she spends out-of-doors, like her brother, and I cannot get her to wear a bonnet against the heat. She cares nothing for being a lady and only wants to ride the horse Clayton keeps in a small nearby pasture. Would that I had Amy here to influence her!

Your Sister,
Abigail

March 16, 1887

Dear Maggie,

Here is a letter we had from George last week. He seldom writes, and this is the only letter we have gotten that is more than a few words. Margaret would ride away and join him if she could. It is hard for me to remember that she is only twelve years old, she acts with such will power and independence. But a lack of judgment still prevails, and she does not act responsibly. It is a combination I fear.

Last week she disappeared, riding up towards the mountains, and did not return until well after dark. Señora Teresa sent her son out to find her, and then Clayton himself rode out. When she came back, riding alone, her hair was undone, her skin darkened from riding out under the sun, and in her hand she held the long feathers of an eagle. If I had not known her for my daughter, I would have thought she was from some tribe, a young Indian maiden or warrior riding down from the hills.

Teresa is certain that Margaret has hidden powers, which make her so unafraid that even the cries of the coyotes do not bring her home from the desert. But Clayton believes simply that she acts without forethought. It does not occur to her that she might put herself in danger.

We have had to hire three Mexicans to help with the alfalfa, but we will get good returns on the harvest. The grape vines and the apple trees give us what fruit we need, and our cows and chickens are productive. We are well provided for. As Clayton's investments grow, we have been able to furnish our house with a hickory cabinet and a four poster bed. I spent many winter evenings sewing imported fabric to make cushions for a couch, while Clayton read aloud from the United States history. Our nights spent this way were quite cozy.

I have sent Irene a note wishing her happiness on her wedding day, along with a few yards of blue silk and a set of bowls from the southwest for her new house.

Your Sister,

Abigail

February 5, 1887

Dear Mother and Dad,

I guess you thought I forgot you with no letter or note since last summer. I am still on the Turnstone ranch in Colorado. We are high up and the winter is cold here, but I am used to it and wear three pairs of clothing. There is a rough cabin we can bunk in with a stove, but I sometimes spend that time out riding, running down the stray cattle to keep them from wandering into the hills or over the river. There are near to twenty of us cowhands, some old and a few young ones like me. The old ones are forever telling stories about cattle drives and wild Indians or some sweetheart, and they play jokes on us like sending us out in the night to bring back some steer that ain't lost.

I guess you have heard about stampedes. There was a big one last August when we were driving the cattle. I nearly got thrown by my horse. Right before that stampede started, everything got quiet like we was out in the desert heat in the middle of the afternoon. The cattle, the horses, you couldn't hear nothing, even no insects or the wind. I believe the world was pausing to think about what chaos was coming. All at once hundreds of them cows started running. They didn't pay no attention to direction. They were all just thundering across the ground any way that they could, and we had to try to turn them all together to keep them from trampling each other to death. I had all I could do to stay on my horse. There was a boy with us, his first drive, and he fell off and got crushed to death under those pounding hooves.

I promise you I will come down there to visit before summer. Maybe in April or May for a week or two. I can take the train. I have enough saved up for the ticket.

Your Son,
George

January 19, 1888

Dear Maggie,

I was glad to hear of Alex's progress at the university. He is a bright young man and will do well in law or business, in whatever he endeavors. Our holiday was gay, filled with excitement and busy with preparations. George arrived December twenty-third with two other young men, all of them cowhands at the ranch George is working on. You can be assured there was plenty of merriment, food, and good company. George's young friends were as sweet-natured as George himself, and both had excellent manners. I cannot picture the three of them driving cattle, with all the whooping and shouting and hard riding that seems a necessary part of that work. I venture that I would not recognize them if I saw them out on the open range.

Margaret was thrilled to have actual "cowboys" staying at the house and sharing our table. She asked every sort of question and spent hours sitting before the fire, listening to stories of cattle drives and ranging, with a deep glow in her eyes. "I'd go back with you, if they'd take a girl," she told them one evening, and, of course, they all laughed.

"Really, I would," she insisted.

Maggie, I believe she would. I am almost afraid she will cut off her hair and try to pass as one of them. Amy thinks her sister will change and become a lady during the next year or two. She relates several stories of young girls at her school who turned from boyish ways as they matured. In Margaret's case, such a change would have to be an utter transformation, and while I pray for it, I am not at all certain it will come about.

Your Sister,

Abigail

June 6, 1888

Dear Maggie,

I have seen Sally Burton. She stopped here for nearly two weeks on her way east. She was traveling by railroad, and Clayton and I rode to the station to meet her. She confided in me that she has had great troubles because of her husband's drinking. There are all kinds of saloons in California where they settled. Her daughter is married to a minister, and they have moved up to Oregon to live. Sally will stay in Virginia for a month or more, as her boys are big enough now to take care of the place. It was good to visit with her, but I hardly did recognize her after all these years. She has gotten heavier, and all her hair is gray.

She had word of Bea Manning, who moved to northern California after her husband died ten years ago. She has her own store, where she sells fashionable dresses, and has joined the suffrage ladies. I do think she is right and that we should get the vote.

You must visit with Sally while she is in Stillwater. I wonder what she will think of the transformations that have taken place.

Your Sister,
Abigail

September 20, 1888

Dear Maggie,

I was pleased to get your letter relating the visit you had with Sally Burton. But I must disagree with you over the causes you found for her hardships. I doubt her husband's behavior would have altered had they stayed east of the Mississippi, and surely that is the origin of her troubles, not, as you put it, "a life spent in the wilderness of California." Let me assure you, the California Sally has settled in is far from being a wilderness. There are large towns with streets and stores, schools and churches, and yes, saloons. But men who would do evil will find temptation wherever they may go.

Let me also assure you that my appearance is not "that of an old woman, completely worn by wind and sun and hardship." My hair is still nearly all yellow, and while I do not look like a young girl, my complexion has not been "furrowed by the elements." I will have my picture made immediately and sent, so that you can see for yourself that the west has not so altered me.

There was a spelling bee at the school yesterday, and it was well attended. Amelia Brown, the minister's daughter, won the prize, which was a bound edition of Tennyson's poems. There will be a neighborhood gathering this weekend, which promises to be lively. I have convinced Margaret to go and wear the new dress I have made her. You see, we are quite civilized here in the west.

Your Sister,
Abigail

April 17, 1889

Dear Maggie,

I was most distressed to hear from Amy that she was delivered early and the child was lost. She says the doctor reports it is a weakness in her constitution, but she was always a strong girl and as a child could work beside me the whole of the day, planting or caring for the little ones. I never knew her to tire.

I telegrammed that I would come east at once to assist her recovery, but today I received a note that she has nearly regained her strength and will return to the school to teach until the end of the year. She writes that I should not leave, especially now just when the planting will begin, and that she and Everett still plan to visit us in June, just two months away. Once again, I entrust her to your care. Perhaps I can convince her to stay with us the entire summer. I believe she needs the desert air.

Your Sister,
Abigail

January 2, 1890

Dear Maggie,

We spent Christmas Eve at the Sloaners' house, which is nearly twelve miles from here. They are homesteading like us and attend the Methodist church. There were ten adults and several children, and we ate wild turkey, pheasant, squash, pumpkin, breads of all kinds, and corn pudding. I brought a dish I had made of the last of our potatoes, and the Porters brought oysters, a rare treat. The house was decorated with lace and pine branches, and there were small figures cut out of paper pressed to all the windows. A tree hung with candles filled the hallway.

Small gifts—handkerchiefs, sachets—were exchanged by all of the ladies. I made Margaret a dress of gray wool, trimmed in bright green, similar to one I saw in the *National Cloak and Suit Company,* with a tight waist, buttoning up the side, which Amy writes is quite the popular sort to wear. Margaret had wanted a new saddle, but if she was too terribly disappointed, she did not show it.

For me this Christmas there were paints Clayton had ordered and a new sketch book. I had sewn Clayton a shirt of white linen, and he laughed when he saw it, as he has little occasion here to wear it.

Maggie, your life sounds so filled with excitement. To have Robert's wedding one month and the following month the birth of your first grandchild. I wish Irene and the baby the best of health.

Your Sister,

Abigail

May 21, 1890

Dear Maggie,

There is a heaviness that will not leave me since I read of Aunt Celia's death. After Mother died, Aunt Celia wrote to me often, filling her letters with town gossip and news of Amy. Just last month she sent me a recipe for a butter cake that is most delicious and advised me to send Margaret away to school. She became, these last years, the mother I lost when I decided to stay in the west. And now she too is gone, lost to me even if I did return east.

This summer the heat has come early. Already, it rises off the desert in waves, by noon turning the land into a sea of red sand. The prickly pears blossom like mad, as if the abundance of light has forced their bright orange and pink outbursts. Our garden is thick with blue verbena. Clayton has bought a parrot from a Mexican, our latest "pet," which he keeps in a cage made of willow twigs hung in the garden.

He claims he will train it to speak English, but so far it only cocks its head to one side and spits out bits of Spanish.

Margaret is fifteen, and I had hoped that by now she would at least show some signs of becoming a young lady, but I am afraid she does not. This spring she has disappeared sometimes for much of the day, taking a horse and riding up into the mountains. Once she was gone for an entire day, and I feared she had run away as George did, but she returned in the evening tired and hungry, her skin burnt from riding out in the open.

She said she got lost up in the canyon, but Clayton fears there is a boy she is meeting. He rails at what he calls her deceptions and threatens to hire a Mexican for the purpose of watching her. Their fights are awful to endure, the yelling and screaming, with Clayton calling her a whore and Margaret accusing him of every sort of cruelty. I should not go against my husband, but I believe, I know in my heart, she is only bewitched by the desert and cannot stop herself from riding all day up into it.

Your Sister,
Abigail

Between Earth and Sky

January 24, 1891

Dear Maggie,

This morning I write to you sitting beside our new cook stove, a Majestic range Clayton bought in December. I have baked seven loaves of bread, which has warmed the damp, drafty house. George was here for Christmas. Last summer he helped bring a herd of longhorn cows up from Mexico and said some of their horns were nearly five feet long and could easily rip a horse open!

"It's time you were settled," I told him.

"Come back home to live," Clayton said, and told him there was land here he could have.

But George is set on working ranches. I guess he would not know what to do with himself here after the excitement of working with the herds. I can only hope he will meet some girl and she will make him settle down. But that is unlikely while he is living among cowhands and the herds.

The night before he left, he came to us and said that Margaret had begged him to take her with him up north to the open range. Maggie, you write that Susan is also strong-headed, but Margaret is sometimes beyond all sense. I had thought she would outgrow the notion that she could live like a boy, but she still has a child's desire to do all that her older brother does.

Soon she will be grown and has received little schooling.

183

A few years ago I wanted to send her away to school, as we did Amy, but she said she would never live in a town, where the houses are close together and where there are always people in the streets. Yet here in the valley she is too solitary, no young women to laugh with, no proper young men to socialize with.

Last spring and summer she often met Señora Teresa Martínez's son, Ramon, when she rode out to repair the acequia. It is a chore she has helped with for years, and quite often they have done it together, as most repairs require more than two hands. She does not understand why, now that she is a young lady, she can no longer accompany a young man, especially one of Spanish descent, unchaperoned. Some mornings they were gone together for hours. Clayton said he would not allow it and often rode out after them. He never saw that they did anything together other than repair the acequia; indeed, they were usually dragging out branches or reinforcing a bank when he came upon them. She has no thought about pretenses or reputation, and she is alone so much of the time, more so than Amy or George ever were. All of her companions are Spanish. She speaks the language without a fault.

My failure has been her education. She cannot sew even a simple hem, and her arithmetic is so poor that I don't believe she could figure the prices listed in a catalog or in a store. When I tried to get her to read to me from the Bible one evening, there were not many words she knew.

"How will you manage your own house?" I asked, but there is no shaming her. She thinks she can live like George does, out in the open on a horse. And she does ride well; there are not many men who ride better than she does. My hope is she will marry some rancher and be content to let him do her riding for her. It is difficult to be a mother of such strong-willed children.

Your Sister,
Abigail

June 15, 1891

Dear Maggie,

Amy and Everett's visit last month was a treat for us. They came in May, she said, because that is when the desert is most beautiful, and we spent many afternoons, and several mornings and evenings, riding through the wildflowers, Spanish broom, which are covered with yellow flowers, the red and orange Indian paintbrush, white-blossoming snakeweed, chamiso, and the cacti, which blaze with large ornamental flowers this time of year.

Everett seemed to enjoy these trips and suggested rides nearly every day up into the mountains or along the mesa. From there, surrounded by red and yellow clay, the small, gnarled piñon trees and prickly pear, you look out across the fields of the valley, which are pale green with the early plantings of alfalfa and corn. Perhaps it is the contrast between the valley and the mountainous desert that makes this place feel enchanted.

"It's a wondrous place you've brought me to," I heard Everett say to Amy one afternoon, as we looked out across the valley, and I imagined for a brief moment how changed my life would be, how wonderfully transformed, if Amy and he moved to this place. But they have made clear, both of them, that they have duties and attachments in Virginia, which they never could leave. I suppose the most we can hope for are their visits, which I assure you I value.

Their two-week visit sped by, and I must confess I fell into such despair the night before they left that I begged Amy to convince Everett to let her stay on another week. She said she herself had commitments back east, but promised that she would try to come back for another visit before her teaching job at the academy begins in the fall. How I long to have her here, but I am thankful, as is Clayton, that they are such an industrious couple. That is the way to success in all things.

Life here proceeds as it has each spring and early summer. We had a good planting, and the river is still high. Margaret seemed pleased to see her sister and went riding with them every chance she got, showing off her abilities in the saddle. Amy tried to impart some wisdom. I heard her lecturing on decorum and the skills one must cultivate to get through this life. She offered to take Margaret back with her for the year, but Margaret would not go, saying she could never live where the sky is hemmed in by trees and buildings.

If only Amy could have stayed on, I am sure she could have altered her sister's perilous course. Clayton says I sympathize too much with Margaret, but she has no sister here, no good friend in whom to confide, and I cannot bear to hear Clayton rail against her.

In some ways it is as if Amy's visits open a wound in me. For many weeks I will long for her company. I wish that I felt as much for Margaret, but I cannot. When the afternoon light hurts my eyes and cuts a sharp silhouette of the bare mesa, I think of Margaret, for this is her desert—the blinding light, the loneliness of the sky. There is a story of an apparition which is sometimes seen by lone cowboys, a beautiful young woman with long, thick, dark hair on a silver-gray horse, who does not acknowledge the cowboys' calls. It is Margaret they see riding out alone, or some spirit that is hers.

Amy does not know the fears I have for her sister, only that there are some concerns. These are words from one mother to another, words from a sister.

Keep them in your heart,
Abigail

November 17, 1891

Dear Maggie,

They have asked me to help teach at the Methodist school. Miss Alden invited Clayton and me to dinner after services last Sunday and asked if I would consider coming two mornings each week to help the children with their lessons. The school has expanded during the last two years and is in need of more instructors.

Pamela Porter, who advised me to refuse the position, does not believe the school can ever succeed at educating the Indian children. Since most of the people in the valley are Catholics, they will not send their children. The children who live on the few farms and ranches settled by easterners often run wild, and so you can imagine the task set before these educators. Most of the boys have their own horses and ride wherever they please. All of them want to get on with a cattle company and live a rough life. There are not many girls at the school, but I fear they are all like Margaret, forever riding across the desert or along the roads that run through the valley. One has to worry about them. Just last week some men got in a fight on one of those roads and a man was killed.

Maggie, what shall I do? I suppose I will go against Pamela Porter's advice and take the position. I am sure I could learn much from working beside Miss Alden, and it would allow me to watch Margaret more closely. Perhaps I can find some suitable companions for her. I have heard of two young ladies recently moved with their parents to our section of the territory.

Clayton claims I am lonely without any little ones to care for. I still wake before anyone else to watch the sun turn the desert red. After Margaret and Clayton are gone and the cow is milked and the chickens fed, if there is no snow, I might take my sketch pad and walk through the cold morning up towards the mesa, ankle deep in sand, my skirts twisting about in the wind. The sun slides across the sky, and I am above the world with it, lost to the clouds that gather along the horizon and sky, sky, sky.

Your Sister,
Abigail

February 12, 1892

Dear Maggie,

This season has been nearly lost in the flurry of my activities. I spend two days a week teaching reading, writing, spelling, and sewing at the mission school. Overall, the change of pace has done me good, and I look forward to my morning rides across the snow-powdered ground.

An added advantage to my position is that I have the opportunity to accompany Margaret to the school and sometimes observe her at her studies. I have given her extra tutoring and watched her reading improve. When I have her attention, she learns quickly and recites with confidence any passage she has memorized. I am hopeful my advice will have some effect on her.

I still do not understand how a child of mine could have become so unlike me, so foreign and unknown. Recently, I discovered her "collections": feathers and stones of all sorts, the delicate bones of a lizard, a dried cactus husk. Clayton is certain that when she disappears for hours at a time she is with Ramon. He has questioned and bullied her, calling her all kinds of names, but she will not say where she goes or if she has been with someone. Neither will she deny his accusations. I cannot believe she has any lover; she seldom speaks to anyone, even at the school, and is so much alone.

Sometimes, despite myself, I envy what sets her apart. It is something untamed, like the wild abandon with which she rides, the brightness in her eyes matched by the hard edge of blue that runs along the horizon. More than any of us, she is a child of the desert.

The Indian children who attend the school are small, with smooth dark hair and bright black eyes. Some of the little Indian girls come to school dressed only in a slip, with a shawl or blanket. The government sends clothing for them, shoes, stockings, muslin, calico, but there is never enough of it.

The teaching that I am responsible for is not nearly as difficult as I had feared. The younger children are a delight, filled with questions and eager to try their hands at tracing letters on the slate boards. There is a young lady who, despite her dark coloring, brings Amy to my mind so surely that at times I have difficulty watching her. She can spend hours with her reader and looks up only once or twice to find the meaning of a word. I have taught her fine lace work and cross stitch, and she made the prettiest collar for a blouse of mine.

The priests continue to do what they can to destroy any good work the school could do. Many of them are corrupt. We know of a man who paid a priest twelve dollars to perform his marriage to a fourteen-year-old girl. With so much corruption in this territory, I am afraid we will never get statehood. Recently, I read in the newspaper that the sheriff and police chief were assassinated by a gang over an election. This did not surprise Clayton, who has long held that most of the politicians are outlaws, but I had a vision of some order, that at least government officials were beyond the violence.

Your Sister,
Abigail

May 29, 1892

Dear Maggie,

Margaret has disappeared and left not even a note to tell us where she has gone. I have searched everywhere, each room of the house. Her bed was made, the spread pulled tight across the mattress. Her clothes still hang in the closet. There is not much she has taken besides her horse, and I was afraid at first that someone had forced her to leave.

But Clayton, certain she had run off with Ramon, rode over to his house this morning and found that he was gone also. Clayton has accused Señora Teresa of being an accomplice. "She is too nervous," Clayton says. " 'Where did they go, Señora?' I kept asking her. And she only shook her head, never denied knowing."

If they have run off together, I cannot imagine where they will go. A minister would not marry them, a Protestant girl and a Catholic, but the priests will do anything if they are paid well.

Clayton has said he hopes she will not return. He claims she has misused every advantage we have tried to offer her and that he watched her behavior these past few years and read the future in it. But I had hoped still for a change. Perhaps I should have been firmer and insisted she go east to live for a period of time with Amy. I fear it is too late now for me to shape her life.

I have not yet written to Amy of her sister's disappearance, as I know it will distress her. Wait to speak of it with her. Maggie, I have lost them all now, every last one. Amy to the east and all the others to the west. I know you are thinking I deserve this, stubborn as I have been to live my life out here and refuse the comfort and safety you and Mother offered. If Josh or Patsy had lived, would they be gone now also, lost to the wilderness of this place, everywhere and nowhere at once in this vast country?

> *Your Sister,*
> *Abigail*

February 2, 1893

Dear Maggie,

Your letters arrive and I have begun several times now to answer them, but the paper gets put away or left beside my chair, where I find it days later, still white and empty. Last summer, after Margaret left, for a time I was despondent and did not care that our cuttings of alfalfa were the largest they have ever been or that corn ripened in the fields, their kernels the color of honey. Even the trees which were thick with apples and the grape arbor strung with heavy purple clusters could not touch the sadness that hung on me when I walked through the house and looked into the empty rooms.

In September Miss Alden rode out to visit and asked if I would consider teaching more classes. After some deliberation, I agreed to teach three days a week, and since then there have been several weeks when I have spent four days at the school. This gives me little time to keep the house cleaned and prepare our meals, but Clayton has taken over with the animals and does the evening milking.

My mornings at the school consist mainly of teaching reading and penmanship to the younger students. The children are eager to learn and full of curiosity. I have had difficulties with only a few of the boys, and when they are disruptive I send them from the class. The Indian children are well behaved, quiet and gentle. The little girls, with their dark hair and eyes that are shaped like almonds, move with uncommon grace. I am certain the sketches I made of them playing in the courtyard will be excellent studies for my paintings.

In the afternoons, I teach sewing and sketching to the older girls. There are a number of "artists" in our group, and most of the girls enjoy embroidery. It is difficult for me to watch the older students who are most like Margaret, those not able to sit still or not interested in completing the tasks laid before them. I ask myself what I might say that would turn them towards a productive path, but nothing comes to mind.

I have gone twice now with Miss Alden to the Indian reservation. They live in white-walled adobes, which they decorate with long strings of bright red peppers. The Indian women adorn themselves with jewelry made of stones that only they seem to know how to find. On festival days, the Indians wear white moccasins and leg wrappings and dance in the streets, waving sticks decorated with feathers and large rattles.

Last month, Señora Teresa brought me a letter Ramon had sent, asking her to see it was safely delivered to me. In it he asks Clayton and me to bless the marriage he has made with Margaret. "He steals her away in the night and then begs our blessing?" Clayton shouted when I read it to him. "Let him beg. They're neither one welcome here."

They have bought a tract of land in Mexico and plan on ranching. Señora Teresa has said there are bandits and all kinds of cattle thieves there. Margaret has always been determined to do with her life as she wishes. I can only hope there is a foundation of good sense laid in her childhood to which she might return.

Your Sister,
Abigail

June 2, 1893

Dear Maggie,

Clayton and I traveled to Santa Fe last month to shop and see the city, for in truth it has grown into a city, with streets which are lined with buildings and the poles that hold electrical wires. We stayed the night in a boarding house just to see the lights come on. For quite some time we wandered up and down the streets, marveling at the glow which here and there filled a dark window. There was a fiesta nearby, and we sat in the courtyard listening to the violins. Clayton held me as if I were a young bride and we danced among the gardens. I felt myself lucky to have such a husband.

The next morning the market was filled with all sorts of people, and one heard every kind of language being spoken. There was a Chinese man selling embroidered silk from his cart, and wagon loads of squash, peppers, tomatoes, corn, apples, nuts, even peaches and cherries. There were enormous jars of beans and strings of prayer beads. On all the street corners Indians stood with their blankets, pottery, and jewelry. It is fashionable to have one's picture taken with the Indians, but one has to pay for this honor, sometimes handsomely, depending on the avariciousness of the model.

After an hour or two the market place had thoroughly confused us with its loud chaos—the shouts of those bargaining, the music of stringed instruments, singing and dancing, the screeches of a parrot, a donkey's brays. We wandered into a stall filled with picture frames of designs made of human hair, yellow, brown, red, black. It was a sight that nearly made me sick, and I thought of the two pale-blond locks of hair I have set in a frame, tucked away with my Bible.

Clayton took my hand as we left that place, and we walked away from the market towards another part of the town, looking for some quiet place to eat our lunch. It was there we happened upon a small gallery that sells coins, various collectors' items, paintings, and photographs. Several canvases were on display, one by our old friend Dr. Mayfield. Clayton pointed it out, his only comment being that he felt my paintings of the desert were quite superior and that I should submit them for display despite the fact that paintings by ladies are said not to belong in such places.

I have few illusions about my paintings. I have given some of them away as gifts, and so a few of them grace my friends' walls. But as I said to Clayton, I remain an amateur. "I'll send them myself, then," Clayton commented as he took down the gallery's address. "Let them see what a homesteader's wife can do."

It is early summer now, and the desert is still blossoming. I ride out with Clayton along the river to see that repairs are made to the acequia. Our alfalfa fields are planted, and there are numerous apples on our trees in the orchard; the season promises already to bring a good harvest.

We are in accord, Clayton and I, in all that we do. Alone now, the two of us on an evening might walk out to the orchard or along the roadside to watch the sun drop down behind the mountains. Some evenings we spend in the garden, exchanging thoughts. "God is here in the desert and in this valley," Clayton said last night. "I would have given up on God had I not come here after the war." And I remembered how much without hope he was when we first came to the valley, his back bent with paralysis from the mining accident.

We looked out where the mountains meet the sky, where the sun had just begun to touch the horizon. "The firmament, Abigail," he said. "The living light of God."

Your Sister,
Abigail

December 30, 1893

Dear Maggie,

I must write to thank you for your kind note and the book that you sent all wrapped in the prettiest paper. I am sorry not to have written before the holidays. Some days it seems I cannot stop long enough to think even of my loved ones, and when I've spent the day reading to the Indian children or riding through the valley, Virginia seems farther away than ever. In a sense, I am grateful, for when this present moment is filled to its wide brim, the past nearly ceases to exist. But I must be mindful of those far away who should be in my thoughts.

George arrived two days before Christmas, having traveled by train from the ranch he is working on in Colorado. Clayton is glad to have his son's company, and they have taken to riding out together each afternoon. They carry their guns with them on the pretext of hunting but do not bring back any game.

At night we sit by the stove and hear stories of cattle drives and roundups. One evening George persuaded Clayton to tell the story of our passage west, but Clayton is not a story teller and the journey sounded so dull by his telling of it and so short, you would think we did nothing but stare at the backs of our oxen for a few weeks.

"There was a child lost," I said when he was finished. "Your son." Then we both told George of the drowning, and I was surprised to hear how much Clayton could call back, each detail, how Josh's hair was nearly dried from the sun by the time the Indian quit trying to make him breathe, how I insisted on changing his wet clothes before we moved on with the train.

George Michael leaves in a few days for Colorado. Clayton and he are gone this afternoon, having ridden up to

Señor López's to see about buying a horse. I wish that one of Amy's visits would overlap with George's. It has been years since they have seen one another, since before Amy's wedding. Tomorrow is the thirty-first, and I will sweep the entire house so that we can begin the New Year clean. Maggie, do not think because you have not heard from me these many months that I wish anything but the best for you and your family. Amy writes that Robert and his wife have had their first child and Irene now has a second. Soon you will have a whole host of grandchildren!

Your Sister,
Abigail

April 7, 1894

Dear Maggie,

I am writing you this letter upon Amy's insistence. I am past putting the losses of my life onto paper. As you know, Amy arrived with Everett last week for her father's funeral. George came three days ago and will stay the summer to help with the farming. It seems I have gotten my wish that they see one another again. He was fifty-four years old. The doctor has said it was his heart, which the injury to his back all those years ago had weakened.

He was buried on our land, beneath the pale-green cottonwoods. The leaves filter the sunlight so that it flickers across the ground in delicate patterns. It is a restful place. In some ways it seems I knew that our time together was limited, that he would leave me to get old alone. But still, when I saw him that morning—for he died in his sleep, with little sign except for a complaint about indigestion the night before—I could not stop myself from falling down beside him, from sobbing. It was Teresa who found me like that, a few hours later when she came to show me where a patch of wild onions grew.

I do not know what life holds for me—an older woman alone on her dwindling homestead, for I shall have to sell some of the acreage. George has promised to stay on to help me get things in order, but he will return to cattle ranching, which is what he loves. Amy will return east. I have written but received no answer from Margaret.

You have not yet written, but I know how the letter will read when I open it. And perhaps I should sell the land and return east with Amy. She argues this case in an admirable way several times a day. But, as you have commented over the years, I am stubborn beyond belief and seem to have gotten myself planted here in all this sand and dry heat, my roots running as deep as the cottonwoods. I cannot imagine looking out from my window and not seeing the mesa in the distance.

And I must ask myself what Clayton would want. He came to love this land the past twenty years. Last month, on a day when the weather was mild, we climbed the mesa. The piñons that cling to the crevices in the cliffs were a deep green against the purple and red rock. Clumps of sage brush and prickly pear covered the hillside. "In another month the cactus will be blooming," Clayton commented, and told me he intended to ride back up there with me so I could paint them in their full color. I'll need to climb that mesa, Maggie, for both of us.

Your Sister,
Abigail

Chapter 7

October 2, 1894

Dear Maggie,

You ask the same questions that Amy asks many times over: "How do you get along?" These have been difficult months, but you need not be uneasy about me. I have managed to keep the house and the better part of the ranch by selling off more of the outlying land. Of the fifty acres I have kept, twelve are close to the river, where the soil is rich and can be planted each summer in alfalfa. Another few acres are planted in apple trees, the very same ones that Amy and George set in with their father years ago. The remainder of the land is just the way we found it, dry sand and clay scattered with cacti and the sweetness of sage brush and a few juniper trees. I have replanted the grape arbor, and this summer the grapes hung in thick bunches from the trellis. There is an abundance here of everything, and so I have given away what I do not use to good friends and neighbors and the school.

Three days a week I travel the ten miles to the Methodist school, where I read to the younger children or correct the essays by older pupils. In the afternoons I teach the girls the fine art of embroidery, and when I bring my sketching paper and charcoal, those who have finished their work join me for a drawing lesson. They say that there are public schools now in some of the larger towns, but we are still dependent on our little mission school for any kind of education.

Miss Jenny Alden is a source of pleasure for me. If I were younger and unmarried, I would strive to be more like her. She rides into the Indian villages and up into the mountains alone, equally at home and unafraid in any world she enters. She has learned to speak Spanish and the Indian language fluently, so she has no need of an interpreter. Some afternoons we two go together, and I marvel at her.

You must see, I am seldom alone, and when I am I enjoy the solitude of my garden, the company of the animals I care for, or a ride to the mesa. Here at the world's bright edge, now without Clayton, I carve out my life as on a precipice but sheltered from the wind, nourished by the sand and stone.

Your Sister,
Abigail

December 23, 1894

Dear Maggie,

Today we began the Christmas celebration at the school. We give the children candy, sing hymns, and decorate a tree with tiny gifts wrapped in tissue, hung from each branch. The children delight in the candies, ribbons, buttons, and other trinkets. I am fortunate to be kept busy with the activities at the school, for they give me little time to think on Clayton and the celebration we would be planning were he here.

The Indian tribes spend the holiday feasting and dancing. Long ago they were forced by the Spaniards to participate in Catholic rituals, but now they do so willingly, incorporating many of their own dances and superstitions into the celebrations. Some of the Indian children will stay through the holidays. They are really very sweet, shy and retiring. Their dark eyes are large and round. I do think they can learn just as a white child can.

Jenny Alden is an excellent teacher. Each day I am impressed again by her enthusiasm and energy. She is not much older than Amy and came here alone to be a missionary in this unsettled place. Her faith and dedication are inspirational. She believes that all people on this earth have the right and the need to be saved by Christ, and she intends to spread the doctrine as far as possible. She sees the Indians as a people needing instruction. Indeed, as she has pointed out, when approached with patience they learn to read as any other child does.

Miss Alden's suggestion that the Indian children be mixed with the white children met with disapproval. In fact, it is still the main topic at the sewing circles and in after-church conversations. Although I am in the minority, I must say that I understand Miss Alden's point. If assimilation and conversion are our objectives, then the Indian children must not be separated out or treated in any way as different from the others.

I will send you the letter I got from Margaret. It is really only a note, but the first thing I have received from her since she left. Pass it along to Amy when you have read it. As you will see, she mentions her father's death only briefly. I wonder if she feels some remorse that he is gone and she can no longer make amends. Perhaps she still hates him. Señora Teresa is afraid Ramon will take up gambling and thieving to get back the cattle that he lost. At times I hope they will return to live in the valley, where they might lead a more decent life, but that would be nearly impossible. Neither the Catholics nor the Protestants would accept their union. It would be easier if he were the Anglo and she merely the dark beauty who bewitched him. But as it is, disgrace will follow her.

Your Sister,
Abigail

Mama,

Got your letter about Daddy, but could not get there for the funeral. We lost most of the cattle we had bought to start the ranch and are trying to see what next. Ramon says you know we are married but you did not say it in your letter. At least you could say that was good and not just the two of us running wild with no license. Finally I get what I want, to live like George, and better because I am boss of myself, but it is hard to keep from losing the cows. I speak Spanish all the time so sometimes English is hard for me to make out. Could you send me some money? We are low here from losing the cattle.

Margaret

March 7, 1895

Dear Maggie,

I was pleased to hear that Susan will soon have her university degree. You are blessed to have four children, all so accomplished. George arrived for a visit in mid-February, and he left yesterday morning. He has been driving cattle north in the fall to Dodge City the last two years, where they are sold. This past September, he helped drive thousands of cattle. Part of the herd was lost during a large stampede and some of it lost to the river, but in all it was called a successful drive.

He is a young man now, Maggie, twenty-five, think of it. He was a mere boy when he left here. Now he has grown tall and has his father's dark hair. Next month he will leave on a cattle drive to Wyoming that will take him the better part of a year, and he may agree to stay on in Wyoming to help establish the ranch. He is to be one of the lead drivers and is quite proud of his position in this cattle drive, which he says will be larger and longer than any he has been on before.

I gave him woolen socks and winter underclothes, as the weather is unpredictable this time of year and the nights will be cold in the north for some time. I also had a book of prayers and verse for him, even though he has never cared much for reading. He promised he would open it sometimes in the evening.

"It will keep you in mind of how to live while you are

in that wild country," I told him. When he goes on the drives to Dodge City, he collects his pay and heads back for the ranch, not like some who stay on, spending all they have made in the bars and saloons. But Wyoming is so far away that I fear for him.

In fact, Maggie, I am loath to admit it, but the night before he left, I begged him not to go on the drive. With Clayton gone and the rest of my children buried or scattered, it is as if the wind that blows across the desert has battered this house until it has swept away all except for me. I do not think I can stand to lose George for more than six months at a time. But his heart is set on going. And I suppose each of my children is only as stubborn as I myself have been. Once they have made up their minds, it is useless to try to sway them.

I remain your sister,
Abigail

April 20, 1895

Dear Maggie,

Pamela Porter held a luncheon yesterday for Miss Jenny Alden to discuss how we might raise money for textbooks, which the school is badly in need of. Our church congregation is still small, with less than fifteen members, but it was decided that we would have several ice cream socials this summer. Pamela Porter has been working two mornings in the school, teaching reading to the younger students. For the most part, our time spent there is voluntary, but I am not in need of money. The sale of the land last summer gave me sufficient funds for my few needs.

If not for my days at the school and my visits with Señora Teresa, this winter would have passed drearily. Several times this past winter I began to make plans to come east for a visit, but there were either the animals I could not find care for or I felt especially needed that week by the school. It is difficult for me to leave, to go against habit, for this place has surely set itself deeply in me. I cannot imagine not waking with the mesa visible through my window.

Señora Teresa lost her husband several years ago, and she too lives alone, but her married daughters live in the valley. "You are lucky," I tell her, "to have them both so near."

I was afraid she would wish we had never settled here, because if not for Margaret, Ramon might have also stayed. But last week when I said this to her, she denied it. "He would have found a way to go, some other girl or a fight." I suppose they are well matched, both wanderers with an eye for trouble.

It is almost as if there is an unspoken agreement between Señora Teresa and me not to discuss their lives, all the possibilities, for we both can guess them and are frightened. Instead we sit and talk of the weather or the planting. I listen to the stories she tells about her youth in this place. We speak a strange combination of English and Spanish to each other, which we have used over the years. I doubt if anyone else could understand it, but it suits us two nicely.

Since George left the first of January, I have had few visitors. Each morning this winter I woke early and went to the barn that Clayton built. Some mornings the wind was so strong I was not able to wedge the door shut against it. But even on those mornings, when the steaming milk froze as it hit the bottom of the pail, I would smell the sweet alfalfa and remember suddenly whole fields of it turned purple just before cutting.

Much of the day I spent keeping the house and barn tight against the cold, reading, sewing, or painting. So you can see why I looked forward to my afternoons at the school, working with the children. Twice I was snowed in and spent the night with Jenny Alden. Late one night she told me of her childhood, how she was raised by missionary parents in Texas and came farther west to settle here on the last frontier. She loves and respects the Indian children, sometimes following them on long rides up into the mountains, and she sees no reason to stop them from participating in tribal rituals.

"My work is not to tear down but to build," she told me. She is satisfied to see the children incorporate her teachings into their thinking.

You asked if I spend much of my time mourning for Clayton. If you mean do I still shed tears or sit bemoaning his absence: I do not. But he is never far from my thoughts. When I milk the cow, I am thinking of his hands, that were placed just so last winter. When I carry armfuls of alfalfa to the barn, I am smelling the sweetness that was woven through his shirts and hair. Perhaps that is part of why I stay on. For if he is anywhere, he is here.

Your Sister,
Abigail

July 29, 1895

Dear Maggie,

Last spring when I wrote to you of Clayton, I did not mean to worry you. I realize that I could move east at any moment I choose and live with Amy and her husband. I also can see plainly that it is my decision to stay here, and that loneliness need not be a condition of widowhood. Perhaps the word loneliness would better be applied to someone in my situation who did not wish to remain alone.

You asked about my paintings. Mr. Wagner, the gentleman who runs the gallery Clayton sent my paintings to more
than two years ago, finally returned them. He commented
graciously on those of the mesa, saying they were the best
of the group. He did not comment on my portraits of the
Mexicans and Indians. I suppose that is because I did not
paint them in costume or feathered dress, the way easterners
expect them to look.

Mr. Wagner has said I should send more canvases for
his inspection, but I will not. He wrote that Dr. Mayfield saw
them and would like permission to purchase one privately. I
sent a letter to be forwarded to Dr. Mayfield, stating that I
was pleased for him to have the painting. The letter of course
has my return address on it. I wonder if he will write to me.
I am curious after so many years to hear from him. I do not
think it would hurt me now, for I am not so disappointed
with how my own life has gone. I am glad that he will have
the painting.

All through May it rained, and so the alfalfa fields have
been high with color and sweetness. The roads in the valley
are lined with wild roses. I have hired someone to do the
cutting for me, but I go out into the field and help with the
harvesting each day. Much of the spring and early summer I
spent repairing the irrigation ditch. Fortunately, I had helped
Clayton often enough that the work was not foreign to me.
In the garden I have planted lettuce, squash, corn, tomatoes,

beans, and the peppers which I have become fond of. Yesterday I canned a bushel of tomatoes and made a basket of grapes into grape juice, which I will bottle this evening.

I am your sister,

Abigail

December 24, 1895

Dear Maggie,

I have spent hours this past month preparing two older students for the exams and teaching the others the hymns and verses of the season. Fortunately, the weather has been benign, enabling me to travel the miles back and forth to the school.

When I woke this morning and realized that Christmas was suddenly upon me, I had no idea how I would spend the holiday, as George is in Wyoming, helping to build a ranch. But then I remembered Pamela Porter's invitation to spend the day with her family and Miss Alden, who will join them for Christmas dinner. I was much relieved that I will be in good company.

I heard from Dr. Mayfield, a brief note stating his thanks for allowing him to purchase the painting and his assurance that he and his wife will enjoy it. Mr. Wagner sent me the money Dr. Mayfield had paid for it, fifty dollars—

can you imagine it?—even though I had never given a price and did not intend to be paid for it. I have sent it back with a note that Dr. Mayfield and his wife are to keep the painting as "a gift from the desert."

Our hopes for statehood have been set back again by yet another controversy, that over the free coinage of silver supported by a number of those with mining interests. I wonder which side Clayton would argue for were he still alive. I have sold nearly all of the mining interests, and so I do not care if there is a silver standard. I wish that we could move more certainly towards statehood. Surely, that is our main hope for an end to the roughness and violence.

As you know, Amy and Everett were here for the month of August. They arrived just in time to help with the harvesting of the fruit trees. Their presence was invaluable to me, although both of them hover over me since Clayton's death, and they would not let me into the orchard on hot mornings for fear that I would succumb to a heat stroke. This seemed a bit preposterous, as I have spent most of my adult life working out-of-doors in all kinds of heat and cold. All summer I had spent the hottest of days in the alfalfa fields. But no matter. She is a good daughter to come and see her mother. When she told me of the advances she has made for the school she teaches in, I was quite proud.

One evening the three of us rode out along the river. The sun had dipped behind the mountains, streaking the cliffs of clay with rose and violet. "How could you leave this?" I asked her as we sat on our horses, staring out across the river and desert and mountains.

"I miss it," she said. "You think I was glad to leave here, but I miss it." And Maggie, I believed her.

Your Sister,
Abigail

July 17, 1896

Dear Maggie,

I was delighted to learn that Amy has been delivered of her first child. Can you meet me the first of August at the railroad station? I am following this letter with a telegram in case you do not receive it in time. It is difficult to believe I am truly going back. By the end of this month, all of the alfalfa should be in, and so I will miss only part of the harvest. Teresa has told me of a responsible man who could look after the farm and see that the beans and corn are brought in as they ripen. Amy wanted me to come later in the fall and stay through Christmas, but there is the school to consider. I am as bound by it as I am to the land. I will plan to stay for two weeks, which feels like such a lot, but I am sure it will be over before I can turn around.

I will see you finally, Sister, and soon. I look forward so to meeting your children and grandchildren. How many are there now, five? I lose count. And Amy writes that Alex may soon marry. I had thought him a bachelor like our George. Meanwhile, I pray for Amy's recovery and the baby's health.

Your Sister,
Abigail

October 7, 1896

Dear Maggie,

Thank you for your letter. My visit was not "a disappointment," not in any way. I enjoyed seeing all of you immensely. It was only that so much had changed—Stillwater, you, John, the children, some who were babies when I left, some I had never seen, all grown. In truth, the grandchildren were, some of them, older than Irene and Robert when I left. And Maggie, I have changed the most. I could not imagine living in the east anymore; everything felt too close and busy, so civilized. I had not thought the ladies would dress so, for every occasion. They would be astonished to see how I live my life here, riding everywhere, putting on a pair of men's trousers to wade into the irrigation ditch and pull out the fallen branches. I believe they thought me odd, and yet to me it is odd to be afraid of riding out alone into the desert or up some mountain.

But never mind, it only served to show me that I would feel displaced living in Stillwater. You commented that if I were to stay longer, through the winter and into spring, I would find I could not leave the wide streets, the gardens filled with peonies and roses, the flowering dogwoods. I could go with you to the sewing group and with Amy to the museum or to the library. I could meet the woman at the school where Amy has taught who paints. This is, I am sure, all true, but I do not know if they would touch the loneliness in me; only the desert does that.

But Maggie, it was worth the trip, and I will do it again, to see you and Amy and to hold wee Ellen in my arms. You say we have gotten too old, but when we were together, I felt I was a girl again, laughing with you over our follies, sharing a story or secret. I suppose Amy is still insisting on doing all of the housework herself. I do hope she will not go back to teaching. She is so like me, to insist on doing all for herself. Watch her for me, Maggie. I will keep her and the dear child in my prayers.

Your Sister,
Abigail

April 7, 1897

Dear Maggie,

All day I have spent on horseback riding along the irrigation ditches, marking in my mind the sections that will have to be repaired. Señor López has offered the services of his sons, at a fee, to help me, and I may accept his offer, as the walls of the main acequia have collapsed in several places and will require major repair. His wife makes excellent sausage, and for years we have traded, my butter for her sausage, once even during a season of drought when we were thick with animosity.

It has been a long winter, with snow for two weeks in the middle of March. But riding out along the river today, I could already smell the sage brush, and the soft pastels of early spring cover the earth. When I got back, late in the afternoon, I brought out my paints and easel and returned to the river to paint them.

One whole wall that runs along the front of the house I have hung with paintings and sketches. As you walk through my front entrance, you see them as they are lined up in the hallway and dining room. I enjoy gazing at them, and it is so seldom that I get a visitor, other than Señora Teresa, that I do not worry what others might think. There are several landscapes, all in reds, yellows, blues, and purples. One of these paintings is nearly all sky, with a few dark mountain peaks.

Also, I have painted the nearby churches and one of
the priests, along with a few of the Indian children. Most of
the charcoal sketches are of the people who live in this area.
Señora Teresa has posed for me, and I made her portrait in
oils for a gift. I like best to draw the children and some
afternoons will sit at the school with my sketch pad while
the students go about their lessons.

Pamela Porter and her husband came by last Sunday,
and I accompanied them to church. I try to attend at least
twice a month, but the long ride does not always seem worth
it when I am alone. Instead I often choose to spend the
morning with my paints or riding out towards the mesa.
Sometimes I recite a verse or sing a hymn, my voice dwarfed
by the long mesa and wide sky. It keeps me in mind of how
small my place is here on this earth.

Your Sister,
Abigail

October 24, 1897

Dear Maggie,

I received a letter from George last month. It seems
Wyoming is such a cattleman's dream, I do not know if I
will ever get him back. He says the fields of grass go on
forever and they are knee high. He is working hard for Mr.

Dunn to establish the ranch, and I don't believe I will see him again for some time. "Go east for the winter, Mother," he advises, stating his concerns for me staying here alone without visitors during the cold.

For the first time since Clayton's death, I dread being so much alone during the long winter months. Last March when it snowed, I was house bound for more than a week and saw no one. Amy says I must come east for Christmas, and perhaps I shall if I can make arrangements for the care of the animals. Meanwhile, I will bundle myself against the cold and, as I watch the first powder of snow appear, dream of pale-green shoots of alfalfa and corn and beyond them the bright flowering of the desert.

Your Sister,
Abigail

February 26, 1898

Dear Maggie,

We have had two snowfalls in the past week, the latest in the form of a blizzard. This morning I had to thaw out the kettle before I could use it, as the stove had gone cold during the night. I heat with coal, which I haul in sacks. It is a dirty heat. Perhaps before next winter I will purchase a gas stove and see how warm it keeps me.

I am in bed this week with a swollen jaw, my face wrapped in a poultice. As soon as the roads clear, I will find a way to ride to the nearest dentist's office and have him pull the tooth. Señora Teresa has offered to do it herself, claiming an uncommon strength and ability in such matters. So far I have preferred to wait out the blizzard, but if it goes on much longer I may succumb to her services.

In early December I rode to the city to take Pamela Porter to the train depot and visit the shops. There on the sidewalk as I left the dry goods store, I saw Dr. Mayfield. He was returning from a call, and so we only had a few minutes to converse. I knew him at once, as he was much unchanged, but I could scarcely believe he recognized me, I have grown so old. He thanked me for the painting of the mesa and was kind enough to remember George and Clayton. "You saved their lives," I told him, and I do believe he blushed.

His wife, he told me, had passed away recently, and I saw how it pained him to speak of her. "Perhaps," he said as he hurried away, "we could visit one another. I long for a trip through the desert. Life in town grows tiring. You are fortunate to live near the mountains."

If he writes suggesting a visit, I would welcome him. I do not see the harm in our seeing one another all these years later. As we said goodbye, he squeezed my hand and said I was an independent lady and that all of his life he would admire me for that.

Am I an "independent lady"? I suppose I have lived my life as one, but I am not sure it has made my life any more enjoyable; perhaps interesting, but not more comfortable. It seems to me that I have spent much of my life alone. While it thrills me to ride up into the mountains or along the mesa, with no other human under the wide sky for as far as I can see, the days I spend closed in my house during a winter storm become monotonous. Diversion is most welcome when it comes, even if it is only Señora Teresa come to bring me herbs or some local man searching for a lost burro.

I suppose these are a widow's sentiments on a long winter's afternoon. As soon as the snow melts I will go out for a ride along the valley and stop to talk with any neighbor I chance to see. And with my tooth mended, I will return to the school, where I am certain they will have missed me.

Your Sister,
Abigail

July 2, 1898

Dearest Maggie,

Your descriptions of your grandchildren playing with little Ellen are precious. I have put all of it to memory by now and recite it to myself when I am sitting alone in the garden in the evening. Evening is the only time that I can enjoy the garden; the heat that blew across the land in May has settled over the desert, heavy and still. The irrigation ditch is low, and I doubt I will get another cutting of alfalfa. I am sure the fruit on our trees will be quite dry and tasteless.

Here is a letter from George. You can give it to Amy to read when you are done. He sounds ready to come back and settle down. I hope that he will. You are fortunate to be surrounded by your grandchildren, Maggie. Last night as I sat in front of the house gazing at the mesa, its dark, looming form against the sky, I thought of Clayton and how certain he was at one time that Amy, George, and Margaret would marry and settle nearby. He saw us both living into old age surrounded by the family we had brought west to raise. Now he is dead and the children scattered. I wonder what he would do if he were me, alone on the ranch.

But I know what he would do—see to the crops and the orchard, mend what is broken (this I cannot seem to do, and so the cabinet doors do not close properly and there is a cracked window pane), feed the chickens. Clayton would go on with his life here, as I have done, without any of the rest of us.

I remain your sister,
Abigail

May 4, 1898

Dear Mother,

Winter in Wyoming is not like winter in New Mexico. We have had several inches of snow on the ground since December, and there are many nights where it is twenty or more degrees below zero. There were a few warm days last week when the snow melted off the fields, but today it is cold again and there are flurries.

Mr. Dunn plans to send up another few hundred cattle next month, and I will stay long enough to get the fencing done and help with the branding. New Mexico sure does look good to me after this winter, and you can count on seeing me before next fall. There are a number of ranches I know of in northern New Mexico, near the Colorado border, and I will find one to work at. I have thought of giving up cattle driving, as I feel so much older than when I started, but I don't know of anything that I could do better.

There is another hand, named Matt, who wants to go south, and we will most likely travel together, if he does not turn wild on me and insist on spending weeks in one of those towns. Some of them do that, they are so starved to know anything else besides the open range and horses and cattle. But I always did love that best.

Your Son,
George

March 15, 1899

Dear Maggie,

Tell Amy not to worry; there is nothing more to do. One of Teresa's daughters, Paula, has offered to help me. She does not expect much payment for this, but I will give her what I can. She is married to José, whom I have hired for five years now to help with the harvest. They have two young children, and Paula is gentle with a baby. If Ramon is the father, as Margaret claims, then the child is Paula's niece.

There is really nothing that I need. Pamela Porter knit a blanket, sweater, and cap, and I have been furnished nicely by several other good neighbors and friends. Señora Teresa comes often to visit and makes much of the "bella bebé." We are a couple of old women easily delighted by any accomplishment the wee thing manages.

Margaret disappeared a few weeks after the baby's arrival. She had asked me for money to pay for a train ticket to California, but I would not give it to her. She had no real plans, just the thought of getting away. It still amazes me that she could leave her infant daughter. Señora Teresa tells me that Ramon is working for a rancher in Mexico. She is afraid he is stealing cattle for this man and says Ramon hopes to marry the rancher's daughter. He seems to have no interest in the child. I suppose he could have his marriage to Margaret annulled with proper payment.

It is a warm spring, the river already flooding its banks with melted snow and ice rushing down from the mountains. The branches of the fruit trees are like pale-green feathers, the new leaves having just unfolded. I could not resist breaking off several to put in a vase so that I can watch the buds blossom. They sit in the back bedroom, in which I have set up an easel. As soon as they open I will do a painting of them, using a stretched canvas and the paints Amy sent me for Christmas.

Your Sister,

Abigail

May 24, 1899

Dear Maggie,

As I have written several times to Amy, I am in excellent health and Paula is quite reliable. I still find time for my work at the school and my sketching, and I attend church and social gatherings. Last year I harvested the apple trees myself, helped with the alfalfa, and managed a small garden. I see no reason for this year to be any different.

There is gossip, of course, but I hold my head quite high and refuse to acknowledge it. Three mornings a week I work with the advanced students at the mission school on their writing. I also teach drawing. I read the newspapers, the books Miss

Alden lends me, whatever I can find. And when I do find myself with a free hour or more, I take out my sketch pad and pencils or I paint. Mr. Roosevelt came to our territory and is reported to have said that if New Mexico wants statehood, we can count on him to go back to Washington and do everything to help us. I am hopeful we will soon become a state.

As you can see, I am quite active, and as ever, my feet are firmly planted.

Yours,
Abigail

December 24, 1899

Dear Maggie,

It is nearly Christmas Day, and the ground has been frozen hard as bone since Thanksgiving. It has been a difficult winter already, the wind like a wedge against the house until the door remains shut most of the day, and I am a bent shape beside the stove, a cup of broth or tea in my hands. This is a holiday, and so I shall try not to be forlorn, but after writing that he would be back in time to spend Christmas with me, George has not posted a word.

Would that I were in Virginia with you and Amy, but then who would feed Elsie, the cow I recently purchased, or

Ginger, a large brown dog who arrived here last fall, slinking around the place like a shadow. And of course, Anna is too young to travel, and as competent as Paula is, I could not leave any baby who has been placed into my care. There is nothing for me but to stay by the stove until it is again time to brace myself against the wind and milk Elsie. Fortunately, Teresa keeps me supplied with baked goods. She is known for the rolls and sweet bread she makes each holiday season. Ginger stays curled by the fire at my feet as I eat these delicacies. I do love her company.

In his letter George wrote that he had stopped in Colorado to visit a rancher he had worked with. While there, he was asked to accompany a posse on a roundup of some horse thieves. They chased those bandits nearly to the mountains before they caught them. I wrote to him suggesting that perhaps he could get on somewhere as a sheriff. It seems to me this would be steadier work than cattle ranching, and he might get to sleep in a bed more often. But I don't doubt it would be dangerous.

Yours,
Abigail

December 29, 1899

Dear Maggie,

George got here two days after Christmas. He came riding up on the prettiest horse I ever saw, almost pure black, with white feet and a white mark on its neck. The ranch he has been hired to run stretches out for nearly twenty miles north of here, near the Colorado line. There is a cabin provided for him, but it was evident that George preferred spending most nights, except the coldest, sleeping outside near the cattle.

"After fourteen years, I would think sleeping on the ground would lose its appeal," I said to him. But he only explained to me again that he does it so that he can hear if the cattle run off. It would not surprise me if George slept that way without the cattle, for it has become so much a habit.

Yesterday I took George to town and bought him two more sets of clothes and a wool blanket. I have ordered him a new pair of leather boots, as the ones he wears have more holes than leather, and I have told him he will have to stay and visit me until they get here.

Your Sister,
Abigail

February 13, 1900

Dear Maggie,

George left the very last day of January. He had said he would leave by the fourteenth day, but that week we had a terrible blizzard, and with the wind blowing the snow up against everything, you could not make out a building two feet in front of you. The snow fell like this for three days, and then the wind wouldn't quit for ten. It was all kinds of silver when we went outside that next week, the sun gleaming across the snow, melting just enough of it to make a sparkling glaze.

One morning after we got Elsie milked and the chickens fed, George brought out our horses and wanted me to ride with him to the mesa his father had loved. It is treacherous to ride in the snow with a sheen of ice across the top of it, but the sun was a big ball in the wide blue of the sky, and I never could resist a ride to the mesa.

There was a long time, maybe an hour or more, where we rode with just the sound of the snow crunching under the horses' hooves. Then George started to talk about his father, and how close they were when George was growing up. They spent hours together in the fields, riding out to repair the ditches, and Clayton sometimes took George with him on his trips to the mines. I never realized how often

George still thinks of his father and how hard it was with Clayton dying when George was just a young man.

When we got to the mesa, it rose up, all powdered white with the dark of the piñon trees showing through. George got off his horse and helped me down, and we stood for a long time, looking up at the strange shape the mesa makes against the sky. The sun was right over our heads, its heat touching everything, and I heard the dripping of water. I thought of Clayton and how he would have enjoyed the ride, but also I thought about the mesa and the desert, how it had been home to me for so long and was as familiar as an old coat or boots.

George is gone now, and I don't know when I will see him again. The baby is well, as hearty as any Paula has ever seen. Perhaps this is due to Teresa's concoctions. She mixes them up in large glass bottles and has me feed them to the little thing.

I have no fears about the child's health; I only worry about what will be done with her. George was angry that she had been given into my care, but I reminded him that I have not yet turned sixty; I am not so old that I cannot care for a child. When I look into her innocent face, it seems a sin that she should have to bear the worst of her mother's indiscretions.

I remain your sister,

Abigail

June 26, 1900

Dear Maggie,

Amy's visit was wonderful. Little Ellen is simply delicious. I could not put her down and got accused of spoiling her at every turn. However, I grew much concerned about Amy. I have never seen her look so tired. Please, Maggie, watch her for me and see to it she goes to the doctor as I advised. Everett seems a kind husband, but he is caught up in his own affairs, more so than ever now that he is running for public office. And Amy is not one to worry others if she is feeling poorly.

During their stay, I instructed Paula to take complete care of Anna so that I would not chance Amy's worry and criticism. Still, she asked me to give up the child. Her concern is all for my good, she assures me. She does not want to see my old age burdened with raising another child. But I cannot give the baby up, and I have money enough from Clayton's investments and the sale of the land to pay for her care here.

The days were perfect while they were here—a clear crisp sky and just the right temperature for riding or sitting out in the garden. Ellen followed Ginger about, and together they chased the chickens. I will miss them.

Your Sister,
Abigail

Chapter 8

December 13, 1900

Dear Maggie,

We had a light dusting of snow last night, and this morning when I looked outside, I was pleased to see the world had moved in such a pretty way towards winter. You must believe me when I tell you I look forward to winter as part of what rotates the seasons and moves the world forward. I do not live in dread of the cold or fear being alone, stranded on my ranch. Indeed, I am not here alone any longer. I have the child to care for. In addition, Paula and José come to the house almost daily to help me with the chores.

In some ways you are right; the child is an inconvenience. I doubt I shall be invited anywhere this year during the holidays. The Porters, the Sloaners, the Deerings, the Browns, all of them find it awkward. They fear if I came for a visit, I might carry Anna with me, as indeed I should, for she is my responsibility. But never mind, I shall spend the season in my own home with little Anna. I find her a delight.

Once a week I leave the child with Teresa or Paula and make the trip to the Methodist school. It is still a pleasure to work beside Miss Alden, and I do enjoy the children. Recently, I had the opportunity to visit with several of the Indian children on their reservation and was able to observe some of the native art work. Their drawings and paintings lack skill in composition, but their use of color in all art work, including weavings and pottery, is quite superior to any I have been able to produce with my oils.

I have read that compulsory school attendance is the law now, but I do not see any indication of it being enforced here. The priests are as active as ever in keeping children from an education. I have heard there are some who insist on teaching in the public schools, and you can imagine that every subject would have a religious overtone. They do not understand the meaning of secular, and they seek absolute control of the curriculum.

I read also what they are saying of us in the east, that if New Mexico is made a state, the priesthood would so dominate as to make successful government impossible. They cite the general lawlessness, also, and depict us as the "Siberia of America." In some ways I must admit their impressions are accurate; however, I still believe our difficulties will be overcome with statehood. Our struggle remains arduous, and no one knows how much longer statehood will elude us.

But do not worry about me. The valley is peaceful, and I am not too afraid to take care of myself. I am an excellent shot with Clayton's gun.

I send you the blessings of the season,

Abigail

February 20, 1901

Dear Maggie,

This has been an easy winter, and despite my protestations of independence, I am glad of it. We have not been snowbound once, and last week I rode out along the river and heard the water running freely, as it does in the spring when all the ice has melted. Such weather could bode ill for the summer months, as a mild winter and early spring often precede a summer of drought and excessive heat, but right now I honestly do not care. I am only grateful that winter seems past and it has been an easy one.

I have received a correspondence from Dr. Mayfield,

requesting the use of one of my sketches for a book he is compiling on the west. I have not had much time to sketch lately but will find some moments, as I would like to give him a number of recent drawings to choose from. He offers to collect the drawing himself, claiming he would enjoy the trip. Maggie, I have sent a note with instructions on finding our farm. I do not care what anyone who knows of this will think. I look forward so to his visit.

The baby does well. She was sickly for several days in January but recovered quickly. I myself was in bed for a few days, and Teresa spent two nights caring for us. She brought with her bags of horehound and spearmint, which she had gathered last spring, and the effects seemed beneficial. For years she has been called a curandera, a woman who is a doctor of herbs. Many of her neighbors have sought her advice. But now that Doña Romero is dead, there are rumors that Teresa is the bruja, the witch. It is because she lives alone since her husband's death and because she is growing old. "Only their mindless superstitions," I said, but she will not speak against them to defend herself.

Last week I received a letter from Margaret. She did not ask about the child, but her questions about my own state of affairs were so insistent that I must assume she wanted some indication of her daughter's well-being. She fled to California, where she has taken up with a traveling band of actors. They are the worst kind in this part of the country, vagabonds capable of every sort of indecency. I only wish that she would return to her home.

Your Sister,

Abigail

July 29, 1901

Dear Maggie,

It seems I have become accurate at portending the weather. We are in the midst of a most terrible drought. I foresaw the difficulties of this season enough not to plant as I usually would, allowing the alfalfa and corn fields to stand idle. And so I have little need for the water that runs so shallow in the ditches and use only what is necessary to keep the fruit trees Clayton planted alive and to grow a few vegetables. Our neighbors bring me corn and grain for the animals. They are grateful to me for not using more of the precious water. Without Clayton, I doubt I would be able to engage in the fight for it; I find it easier not to have the crops that would demand a greater use.

You mentioned Amy's concerns in your letter. Of course, she has written to me also, explicating her reasons once again why I should sell the land and come east this summer. Perhaps it *has* become too much for me to manage. But both of you forget that I have a grandchild and two other children here—George, who wrote last month that he plans to come for a visit in the fall, and Margaret, who is wandering somewhere in California. Although I spend much of the year alone, I must be here for them when they do come home. Clayton would want it. And he would see my return as a failure after all that we worked so hard together to achieve.

Thomas Mayfield visited me here one day last week. We rode along the river and then out across the desert to the edge of the mountains. The mesa loomed over us, its dark, unchanging shape. Thomas wanted to take the horses up into the mountains and ride along the high, flat ridge, but it felt as if that would be a betrayal, for riding along the top of the mesa was Clayton's favorite ride, and so I told him it was too late in the day. "Another time, then," he said, and perhaps there will be a time when I am past betrayal, past the sense that I owe an allegiance still to Clayton.

But Maggie, Thomas has changed, he is not the same young man I knew at all. And why did I not expect it? He has grown so quiet, so lost it seemed in his own thoughts, that I hardly dared speak, and indeed he said little the entire time we rode. But still he would jump off his horse to look at a plant or rock or to rub the sage brush between his hands, his face suddenly animated as it was more than twenty years ago, as if he is still surprised by the world.

He took two of the sketches I showed him for his book, a landscape and one of an Indian child. I have a whole series of drawings of the Indian children and will enclose one in this letter. I gave him another small painting, of a branch of apple blossoms, which he admired.

He gave up his medical practice several years ago to care for his wife, who died of diabetes. Shortly afterwards, one of his sons was shot and killed by a bandit. He has a daughter, who is attending medical school back east, and another son, who lives in New Mexico and has married a Spanish-speaking woman. I told him about Anna, and he said that he has a grandchild who is dark also.

I rode out with him to the railroad station, where he took the train that travels daily to Santa Fe. Before he left, he asked if he could come out another time for a visit. "Of course," I told him. "I would welcome it." And I would. Then he put his arms around me, for a brief moment, there at the station where anyone could see. I did not care. I could feel how thin he has become, how much older.

Your Sister,
Abigail

December 1, 1901

Dear Maggie,

Margaret was here for two months this fall. To put it plainly, she had gotten herself mixed in with the wrong sort of people. She had taken up with a man who ran a theater company. She arrived at the door one evening with only a small trunk, having taken the railroad car from California. She showed little interest in the baby after arriving and only went to her old room and began unpacking her trunk.

"What are you here for?" I asked, following her into the room. "What do you want?"

"I came to rest," she said simply, and rest she did. There was nothing would get her out of bed—not hunger, not the sound of Anna's cries or even the promise to let her have a horse with which to ride out into the hills.

"It is my opinion you've come here to die," I said after two weeks of her lying in bed with the shades drawn.

"I came to forget," she said, then told me things I did not want to hear about the man who ran the theater company and how he took each new girl that joined their company and expected Margaret to clean up after them. He forced her to do all kinds of vile things for him, and when she would not, he turned her out of the rooms where they were staying, so she had to wander the streets, and sometimes with little clothing on.

What could I say to her, Maggie? I gave her your name, and it should have made her sensible and steady of heart, as you are, but she has always had to get just what she wants and there is no thinking on it. "Why did you stay with him?" I asked her.

"Oh," she breathed out. "He was so fine-looking."

I did not raise her this way. That next morning I offered her my plan, that she should stay with me and finish her studies. If she did well, I would send her to a college, so she could teach as Amy has done. "You must find a way to make your own living," I told her, as no man will marry her now. Someday, I hoped, she would be able to take over Anna's care.

At last, she came to her senses and got out of the bed. When I came home from the school, she had dressed and gone outside to see the horses. The next day she held Anna and fed her. Later that week I would hear her singing Spanish lullabies and think: Yes, how she loves her daughter. Like any mother. Each night I tutored her, and she could not get enough of learning, the two of us up until dawn, bent over the books.

"My head," she said once. "It's like being filled with the wind, knowing all this."

Two months she studied and mothered Anna. Oh, she took such care of her daughter at times, dressing and feeding her, playing and singing. A few times each week we would take two of the horses and ride out into the desert or along the river. She asked to do this even when it was bitterly cold or if there was snow on the ground.

Late one afternoon as we rode, the dark hulk of the mesa looming above us, the sky cold and dry, brittle as if it could be cut away like crystal, we heard a sound like the playing of a flute. It was far away but, like smoke, seemed to sift through us. "We need to turn back," I said to Margaret.

Slowly she turned around on her horse to face me. "I love it. Don't you understand?" she asked, and rode off towards the strange music. I would not have been surprised to see her horse leave the ground, she was so fast. It was as if she vanished. Hours after I returned, she rode back through the darkness of a new moon, her hair matted from the wind, tangled and torn like an animal's. And I thought again, as she collapsed on the ground, undone with exhaustion, how she was possessed by some spirit, some animal spirit. She would have slept, slowly freezing, if not for José, who carried her to her bed.

Two days later I woke before the light came under the curtains, and even in the dark quiet I could feel what was changed. When I stepped out into the garden, a cold wind snapped me almost in two. I leaned against the doors to bolt them, and it was then that I felt the chilled stillness which filled the inside of the house.

Anna, still in her bed, felt it too, for she cried out, and

this was my relief; that my daughter had not taken her child. Here was Anna in her bed, not blown across the mountains to some unknown desert, some foreign place. I carried Anna into her mother's room, where the simple shapes of the furniture lay like shadows, and slid my hands along the wall and the bed. The mattress was bare. When I lit a lantern, I saw she had taken her trunk and the bedding with her. Later I would find one of the horses and a wagon missing.

Today the cold finally broke. I should be grateful for the time I had with her, as I was for Josh and Patsy's brief stays, but Maggie, I am not. I wish she had never left California, and if she dies somewhere out in the open, I hope I do not learn of it.

Your Sister,
Abigail

June 12, 1902

Dear Maggie,

We had a quiet winter and spring, with few visitors— Miss Jenny Alden, Paula and José, who came almost daily to help me with the chores, and Teresa, who often spends the afternoon with us. Jenny Alden visits frequently, and twice during the winter she spent the night with us. I delight in her company, for it is a pleasure to exchange ideas with someone who is knowledgeable and thoughtful in all that she does. She brought with her a book by Rudyard Kipling and left it for me to read. Also, there are some papers she is compiling on Indian life from her own observations, which she wished me to read.

Pamela Porter, Annabelle Sloaner, and the others who once formed an intimate circle with me no longer visit here. I know it is because of Anna, but they will not say, any of them, when I ask why they have refused an invitation to dinner or for sewing and gossip. I do miss their company, but their absence has made me value Jenny Alden's company all the more, for she is forthright and honest about her opinions and does not allow any prejudice to stand in the way of friendship.

I look forward to my visits with Teresa with increasing gratitude. We ride or walk the short distances between our houses and talk of Anna, who is her delight, of gardening, the season, young people—of whom we have little under-standing—and water, always the talk of water or drought, about which Teresa has many stories and predictions. She claims this summer the harvest will be plentiful and that the river will swell with water. This she says she knows from watching her burro and horse, for they cannot seem to get enough of running through the pasture. "God tells the animals," she said yesterday as we watched her horse leap across a fallen tree, then rear back on its hind legs as if dancing.

I was sorry to hear of Sally Burton's passing last winter. Amy mentioned it in her letter and said the funeral was held in California, but she did not include any other details. If you know anything more about the circumstances of her death or about the family she left behind, please let me know. I only saw her once since we separated from the wagon train all those years ago, but she has been forever in my heart, as you are, Maggie. I still receive an occasional letter from Bea Manning. She has asked me more than once to meet her in San Francisco, where she travels to do business, and I suppose that someday I shall. It would be quite a reunion that we would have.

Your Sister,
Abigail

January 7, 1903

Dear Maggie,

It was a fine holiday, as full of people as I have had in years. George was here for a week-long visit, and Jenny Alden stayed with us for two nights. All of us attended church on Christmas Day, and it was the first time I have done so in years. Anna was dressed in white ruffles with a wide sash, and Jenny Alden had curled her hair so that it fell in ringlets. She made a pretty picture; even Pamela Porter and Annabelle Sloaner had to smile at her.

George has offered to return in the spring to help build a house for Paula and José here on my land. For several years now José has overseen the planting and cutting of alfalfa and corn. His wife still helps with Anna, and both of them have seen to the chores for me in the winter when I have needed their help. I have paid them, of course, but it is a small amount when compared with what they have given. The house and the piece of land surrounding it are only what they deserve, and as more of the work here becomes difficult for me, it will be necessary to have someone to take over the operations of the farm.

I still work at the school once or twice a week while Teresa cares for Anna. Recently, others have offered to relieve me of that responsibility, but I am not ready to give it up. It is as if those hours exist in a glass that I could carry to the window and, holding it to the sun, watch rainbows dance. Each loss of my life is forgotten, every trial disappears, as I listen to the children recite and watch them compose their lessons. Miss Alden has had her way, and so there is no separation between the white children and the Indians. For the most part it is a harmonious blend.

I have received a letter from Margaret postmarked Arizona. It is really just a note and difficult to decipher. Tell me what you understand of it. I am afraid her mental state is precarious. I have written back that she can come and live with me, as I imagine she is destitute. It is both my hope and my dread that she will do it.

Your Sister,

Abigail

This is a post office box where you can write me, care of Joseph Larnes. I want to know how Anna is and tell me everything. I am staying different places. There was some work but none now. I was trying to get out of California and a bad time there that I came here. I want somewhere to stay but there is nothing to do here not even laundry that I can find. I won't stay in one of those asylums. Oh Susan did and she said it was worse off. I need a horse and then I could ride the desert. Margaret

August 13, 1903

Dear Maggie,

Each summer seems to go by more quickly. If I live past seventy, I suppose I will blink my eyes and the harvest will be over. José managed all of the alfalfa cutting and harvesting this summer. He and Paula are content in their house, which George helped build this past spring. "The land could still be yours," I told George one afternoon while he was here. "I would sign the deed over to you today if you wanted it." But he is used to the wider spaces where they range cattle and says the mountains are too close here. Like Clayton and me, he wants to make his own way.

Anna continues to thrive. Paula tends to the child as if Anna were her own, and Teresa will often keep her for the better part of a day. I sometimes think she receives too much mothering, but I am just as guilty. Entire afternoons I spend with her in my lap, both of us napping. Perhaps I am getting old. Teresa insists I am still young. She herself turned sixty this past summer but still oversees the operations of her farm. Last month I found her in the heat repairing a break in the acequia. "Help me with the wood," she called up to me, and so we were two nearly old women dragging a branch up out of the water.

It has been a dry month. There was little alfalfa in the last cutting, and since most of the water has gone to the alfalfa field, the apples are woody and tasteless. Amy has written that they will visit in October. She sent a photograph of Ellen, which is simply adorable. My hope is that George can get here, if only for a few days during their visit, as they have not seen one another since Clayton's death.

I spend much of my time painting the mountains and cliffs, Paula bent over a child in the yard, a vase of verbena. Are we to feel wise as old age approaches? I cannot imagine it.

Your Sister,
Abigail

January 15, 1904

Dear Maggie,

For nearly a month now, I have meant to respond to your Christmas greetings. As you have no doubt heard, George was here for three days during Amy and Everett's visit. I insisted on taking them up to the mesa, as the month of October was strung with clear, dry days. Amy and Everett were certain the trip would tire me, but it did not. Indeed, poor Everett had more difficulties than I did with staying on his horse. It was during that week in October when the world turns all shades of gold and red, so that it looks as if the land is on fire. The wide blue sky formed a brilliant contrast, which all afternoon I spent delineating in my mind so that sometime later I could paint it.

By the end of their visit Ellen followed me about the place quite merrily and wanted paints of her own whenever she saw me at my easel. I set her next to me with paper and charcoal, and she spent an hour or more at a time carefully marking lines. I do think she has a talent if Amy will indulge it.

Christmas was rather dreary, as a freezing rain fell all day. I am quite sure the ice damaged the fruit trees, and it may have killed the small ones, which I had José plant last fall. The mission school put on a pageant, for which I sewed all of the costumes. Jenny Alden has taught the children to sing beautifully.

While Amy was here, I took her to the school, and she was impressed with the changes that have been made. She said that in reading and writing it was as advanced as the schools back east. The friendship between her and Miss Alden was instantly made. If Amy had not met Everett and settled in Virginia, I can picture her working here, like Jenny Alden, forging a place for young minds in the wilderness.

Anna does well. We had a scare with her last month when she ran a fever for three days, but it appears she only had a cold. Please give Irene my best wishes on her latest arrival.

Your Sister,
Abigail

June 25, 1904

Dear Maggie,

The summer heat is upon us, and the season promises to be dry. Already the ditches are shallow. I have given over the alfalfa planting and harvesting mostly to José. I still tend to my flowers and a small vegetable garden and ride out to inspect the ditches and orchard, but José completes any repairs that must be made and helps with the fruit harvest.

The Reverend Brown and his sister have suggested that I allow them to find a more "suitable" home for Anna, "a good Spanish family." They also offered to raise the child at the mission. I must remind myself that they are trying to be helpful, but she is my grandchild, and I am most capable of making decisions concerning her well-being.

Pamela Porter and Annabelle Sloaner, along with, I'm quite sure, all of the ladies of this valley, believe I have no business raising the child. What they would have me do with her is not clear, but as soon as I enter a room at school or at church where they stand conversing, they are outspoken about their feelings on racial intermingling and the ill that will come of it. Perhaps they fear she will marry one of their own grandchildren when she is grown. Just yesterday, Pamela Porter expressed that it all might seem more acceptable if I were more outwardly concerned, by which she meant more visibly repulsed by the child. I suppose then I could play the martyr.

I still plan to teach this fall at the mission school one morning each week. I attend church each Sunday I am able to make the trip, and I hold my head high.

I remain your sister,

Abigail

December 7, 1904

Dear Maggie,

As you may have heard, George and Margaret were both here for a visit in early November. George had written that he would come just as soon as the cattle drive was over and spend two or more weeks making repairs on the house. Margaret's visit was a surprise to both of us. She arrived late one morning, having arranged a ride with a stranger from the train station. I do not know where she got the money for the ticket, as she came with nothing.

For some time George has been critical of my handling of his younger sister, claiming I should not allow her to come and go, visiting the child when she desires. But she was quite enamored of little Anna, carrying her about the house, singing to her in Spanish, taking over the largest portion of her care, so how could I do as George wished and forbid her access to the child as long as she refused to take responsibility for raising her? He claimed I must take part of the blame for her vagabond life, for I have made it too easy for her to wander about.

One evening, thinking he was partly in the right, I helped him to confront her with her behavior. An argument ensued, in which George told her she was no longer a child and needed to settle down and take responsibility for what was hers.

I will never forget how she turned towards him, her eyes narrow and with a low hissing sound, as if she could kill him, her own brother. "You're the worst kind for that," she told him. "Riding wherever you please, without a care for anything but your own pleasure. I've met some like you and had relations with them. I know the sort you are."

"What are you saying?" he said, shoving her hard up against the wall, whispering so that I almost could not hear him. "That you've worked at one of those saloons?"

I did not hear what she answered, but the next thing, he stepped back and spat on her, then walked out of the house, and we stood there, the two of us listening as he rode away.

Maggie, I said nothing to her. As children, she and George spent entire days together, running across the fields and riding into the mountains. I could think of nothing, as if my whole mind was filled with the darkness that was starting to settle over the earth, for it was late in the day when all this happened.

By the time George returned that night, Margaret had gone. When I saw she was in her room, gathering her things, I found José and asked him to take her to the train station. Before she left I gave her all the money I could spare and a good dress I had bought for her. I have not told Amy of Margaret's abrupt departure, but Maggie, I do not know what else I can do for her. She is gone now, as if she has been carried off by the wind. I have no idea where she will be blown.

George stayed on a few more days, repairing the roof and sealing the windows and doors. We said little to each other. I was bewildered, and in truth, I reproached myself for allowing her to be turned out of my house in that way. However, if she had stayed on, she would have disappeared eventually, and in the end I would still be left with no clue as to where she might have gone. When George rode back north, he left an envelope on the table, with money in it. "For care of the child," it said. I believe he felt remorse also over how it had ended.

Maggie, I cannot believe she is my youngest daughter. Sometimes it seems as if she too is dead, and all I can do for her is raise Anna as best I am able.

Your Sister,
Abigail

April 4, 1905

Dear Maggie,

I know I should sit down more often to compose a letter to send east. Amy writes that you are all filled with concerns. We have acquired two more dogs, a brown one and a black one. They arrived during the winter, half frozen and starved, but are by now filled out and quite at home in the kitchen, where they spend most of the day by the stove.

I have heard that in the cities some people have indoor plumbing and telephones put in their houses. Amy writes she now has an indoor bathroom with its conveniences. Have you had occasion to use a telephone? If so, you must tell me what it was like, as I cannot imagine. I am sure it will be some time before there are men stringing wires across the desert.

The children are well and growing. Paula is forever chasing them about the yard, and I delight in watching them tumble over one another as they run wild and silly as chickens let out of a pen. Anna scrambles with all of them, ripping her pinafores, muddying her skirts, so that I let Paula dress her in play clothes like those her own children wear. It is natural that they play together, for as you seem to forget, indeed as I am sure you would like to forget, she is very much like Paula's children. Her coloring is quite dark.

All winter we were chilled by a freezing wind. In February, when it rained, the ground turned to smooth, shining ice, and I could not walk to the barn but had to ask José to do all the milking for me. On the coldest evening, an old man came to the door with a brass bell tied to the handle of his cane and black rosary beads. I gave him a cup of warm

milk and a plate of meat Teresa had cooked. He told me I
would have a long life, not a difficult prediction, as already
I am old, and then stumbled out into the cold. Teresa says
he is a holy man and that once he touched a blind woman
and instantly she could see. The next morning the cold broke,
ice dripping upon the ground. Soon the valley and deserts
will blossom, and so again the world will be transformed.

You ask about the school. Miss Brown and the others
voted not to have me teach there anymore, which is just as
well. I am occupied here with Anna and overseeing the alfalfa
crop, the orchard, and the animals. I do miss the children
and the few friends I had made there. Last Sunday when
Reverend Brown shook my hand as I was leaving the church,
I saw Pamela Porter step aside and begin talking with Mrs.
Crompton so that she could avoid me. Her behavior is aston-
ishing to me. We have been friends for years, but she cannot
forget the color and circumstances of the grandchild I am
raising in my home.

Jenny Alden is the only one connected with the school
and church who has the courage to stand up against the
popular prejudice. She was outspoken in her disagreement
with Miss Brown's decision, and she continues to speak with
me on Sundays and frequently rides out to pay me a visit.
"We must answer only to God and our own conscience,"
she has told me. She advises me to bring Anna to the mission

school, but I may decide to school her myself, as I do not think I can bear for her to suffer the gossip that will surely surround her.

Your Sister,
Abigail

October 16, 1905

Dear Maggie,

I have meant for some time now to respond to the letter you sent last summer. You must not concern yourself so much about Anna on my account. I will not be persuaded to "give her up now that it is clear Margaret can never care for her." I do not care that I have become "isolated" from my friends because of her. The experience has taught me to see them for what they really are. I have a great affection for Anna and cannot imagine my life without her living here in this house, sleeping in the room where her mother once stayed. I have lost them all; those that are not dead are scattered across the country. I will not be denied the raising of my granddaughter.

I do not care anymore what anyone thinks of me, if my old friends scorn me because the grandchild I have chosen to raise is dark-skinned and born out of an improper union.

And I do not care about propriety. It seems I am too old, too much of my life gone. When I traveled to Santa Fe during the harvest to oversee the selling of the alfalfa and corn, I looked up Thomas Mayfield. He was not there when I rang the bell at his home, but I left a message, and later he came to the hotel where I was to stay the night and asked if I would share dinner with him.

I told him I had ceased caring what anyone else thought of me and that I have few desires left but I wanted his friendship. Then we talked of the desert and riding and of the book on the southwest he has nearly finished compiling. I told him about my painting and about Margaret and Anna and the alfalfa cutting and the orchards. He talked of his wife and the hospital and his son who was killed.

We drank our coffee, and it was nearly eleven. The restaurant was closing as we stepped out into the street. "After I found Clayton and left for the east coast, I was certain I would travel around the world or discover some new medicine or cure or be the first white man to walk through some ancient ruins," he said as we stood under the yellow-colored light from the street lamp. "There was a whole continent, but I came back here and married and set up a practice, trying to get back what we had planned." He looked down at the pavement, up into the light, everywhere but at me. "You went on in the face of everything."

I took his arm and said I wanted to walk. The city's

square was lit with restaurants and saloons that were still open. In just a few hours the farmers would start setting up their wagons for the market the next morning. "I want to stay with you tonight," I said when we had walked nearly half an hour, circling the center of the city and back up along the street where he lives. "I don't care how old I am or about guilt." And I followed him into his house, where there was a bed of solid, heavy oak with the silhouette of a cactus carved into the head board.

I left Santa Fe the next afternoon, having sold all of the alfalfa and corn. He has sent a letter asking if he could come this month for several days. We will ride under the cotton-woods, which have turned the most brilliant shade of yellow, and climb up into the mountains. He has said he will bring his sketch pads and notebooks, and perhaps he will let me paint his portrait. We'll wander out into the desert, and I'll be grateful that I am old and live alone under the hard blue sky.

Your Sister,
Abigail

January 20, 1906

Dear Maggie,

The guarded comments in your last letter about love that "comes too late" being better left alone are transparent. You are right when you say, half humorously, it seems, that I have become more determined and less likely to conform to what is "thought to be right" as I have grown older. "An unusual circumstance," you say. "For most of us mature into a sense of morality."

Thomas was here for several days in the fall, and I have promised to travel to Santa Fe this winter. As soon as I can arrange for Anna's care, I shall. My morality is not based on popular opinion. You write that selfishness belongs to the young, but mine is a selfishness born of age. I am impervious to any criticism.

George visited in November and he repaired the roof, so we stay warm and dry inside the house. He brought with him a graphophone from his latest trip to Denver. I could not have believed the invention of such a machine had I not seen it myself. He played me an opera. It was delicious. He also brought me clothes such as they are wearing in the city, a new hat, a skirt of dotted swiss.

Already we are having a difficult winter, with several inches of snow covering the ground. In the afternoons I bundle Anna, and we walk through the snow to Teresa's house, which smells of cinnamon, anise, and cloves. Plates of *molletes, sopaipillas* (the sweet fried cakes), chocolate, and puddings are lined up across her table. There are pots of ground meat for sausage and piles of the corn husks she wraps for tamales. Anna in an apron is her little helper, rolling out dough, filling the sausage skins. Bunches of herbs and bags of leaves hang from the ceiling. In the corner, a pile of ripe pumpkins. If she is a bruja, it is a good magic she practices. I would hate to live without it.

Your Sister,
Abigail

May 5, 1906

Dear Maggie,

I read in the newspaper the reports of the destruction of San Francisco by an earthquake and descriptions of the burning city. It is impossible to conceive of the lives lost, and I wonder how many of the names of the dead I would recognize, as a number of families from our wagon train all those years ago settled in that area. The Holmeses and the Snellings, the Millers. You would know the names also, Maggie, their descendants strewn from east to west, difficult to trace such a scattering. And Margaret—I cannot keep myself from wondering day after day where she has gone, if she could be buried beneath some building, inside some open crater in the ground.

Last week I accompanied Teresa and Paula and the children to a church some two hours ride from here. It was a small chapel at the foot of the mountains, made recently famous as hundreds have come to see the miracles that are claimed to have happened.

A statue of the Virgin Mary stands in the church yard, and there are some who report they have seen actual tears fall from her clay eyes. Every kind of healing has been laid claim to at this place, all attributed to the weeping statue. While we were there we saw numerous pairs of crutches left by those who no longer needed them, and we heard reports of blindness that had been cured and arthritis and heart trouble.

Paula and Teresa knelt on the ground and would have stayed that way through the afternoon and into the night had I not been there to remind them of the children, who would need to sleep in their beds. I envied them their devotion. "Pray for your daughter," Teresa admonished me, and I tried.

The statue was the size of an ordinary woman, her dress and veil painted bright blue, her hands, face, and feet the color of clay. Her fingers touched in the motion of prayer. No tears fell from her round, blue eyes, but sorrow was so deeply carved into her face that I looked on her and felt I would weep. All that I have left behind seemed embodied there.

Numerous gifts of flowers and food, even coins and a stringed instrument, were placed around the statue. Paula had brought a finely woven basket filled with fruit. Teresa had brought a bowl painted with butterflies. I wished suddenly that I too had carried something, and so I left the small silk change purse from my pocket.

It was late when we left for our valley, and we rode the last hour home through the dark. I was afraid the horse would stumble on some rock or the wagon turn over an unseen embankment. The children slept, and all three of us were silent, staring across the land, which after dark stretched away from the road like fields of black water. Then Teresa began to weep, sobbing so forcefully I was afraid she would wake the children. But her sounds were hollow against the night, which poured out everywhere as if the sky had split and the dark, star-speckled ink ran out. It would have brought me comfort, a measure of relief, to have joined her.

When we reached home, the children were still asleep, all except for Anna, who wanted to know how a statue could help someone to walk again or see. I wanted to tell her about God, I should have explained Catholicism, a faith that does not follow reason, but instead I told her about art, that a statue, like a painting or drawing, can never be more than a mere representation.

"Even if it cries tears?" she asked.

"We did not see any tears," I reminded her. "And if we had, if indeed others have truly seen the statue weep, it means only that the work of art is so well done, it comes so close to being the actual person, that we look on it and believe we see the tears. That is the power of art, to change our vision, to make us see what is not there."

Anna kissed me on the cheek; she went to bed. In the evenings I watch her running through the orchard, so light on her feet she could be dancing, and I think for a moment how like her mother she seems, moving everywhere at once. But as soon as I think this, she runs across the field and lies on the ground at my feet, more pensive than her mother was, more practical. She says she is sure it is time she was in bed. "Like a little adult," I tell myself. "Already, like a little mother."

Your Sister,
Abigail

October 25, 1906

Dear Maggie,

We have started riding, Anna and I, up into the mountains. Last week we rode beneath the long, flat mesa, and the sky suddenly tore. Clouds twisted against the flat blue in every sort of shape, gray mushrooms, thick bulbous creatures. The wind rushed between branches of the piñons and fir trees, blowing sand into our faces. Dark clouds knotted, and long, feathery plumes swept the sky.

We dismounted and found a small cave. From that hollow place cut into the side of the mesa, we watched lightning strike so close we could smell the burnt, sulfuric odor and see the sparks that grazed the piñon trees. Maggie, I wanted to weep with fear, but Anna reached out, she held my hand, and we stood watching until the storm had passed.

Later as we walked back I told her how brave she had been. "We need the rain," she said simply, and it was true, we were in the midst of drought.

Do not worry that we are too surrounded here by the Catholics and "their miracles." Anna will make her own way. Unlike her mother, she is a sensible child. Her feet are firmly planted.

> *I am your sister,*
> *Abigail*

January 15, 1907

Dear Maggie,

I know how difficult, how peculiar my life must seem to you. You say that I must accept age and not act as if I am a young woman. I am sixty-seven, but I can still climb up into the mountains. If it is foolish for me, "an old woman," to do so with a child, so be it. I cannot stop myself from going.

You write that Amy has concerns that age is beginning to make me "senseless." The two of you have talked of this. "Perhaps it is too many years in the desert, too much sky, too much wind and sun. Did it not make Margaret mad?" you ask.

If Amy has worries about my mental condition, she did not tell them to me when she was here at the end of last summer. Instead she asked me to take her riding and praised the food Teresa brought. After the first day, she did not even try to convince me to give up Anna.

You ask why I do not marry Thomas Mayfield if we "must" persist in visiting with one another. It is because I prefer to continue living here alone. I am used to running the ranch, to the hours when Anna is with Paula or Teresa, which I spend painting. I see Thomas whenever I like. I do not care how you or Amy or anyone else might judge me. (I have not told Amy, so if she knows, it is your doing.) Teresa says it is because I am getting old that I have stopped worrying over what the rest of the world might say. Raising Anna has taught me that I cannot care, and I thank the grievous circumstances which brought her into my life.

You say you are concerned only for my good. Go on praying for me, Maggie, as you have said that you do.

Abigail

September 15, 1907

Dear Maggie,

Each morning this season I go to the orchard to pick apples, for we are having a harvest like none we have had in years. All morning, leaning my ladder against the trees, I climb into their deepest centers, into the cores where leaves thicken and the fruit hangs heavily off the branches. There, reaching upwards from my precarious perch, I close my hands around the hard red fruit. The sky is down among the leaves, and surrounded by the low hum of bees, I grow thick with light.

Sometimes as I stretch towards the fruit I think of you, Maggie, so many miles away it seems I will never reach you, and I wonder how I could feel so much anger at your accusations about my grandchild and Thomas, mixed with the longing I feel for your company. There, among the leaves and fruit and sky, in all that dappled light, my objections seem inconsequential. They are not worth risking the tenuous connection our letters have strung together these many years.

Is it tenuous, Maggie? Today I feel that it is, yet at other times it has felt as permanent and binding as any tie could be to this earth. If we were to lay out our letters, would the link seem more substantial? Would the letters themselves provide some sort of order to our experience, a concrete way of understanding our lives? Or would we be lost still in the details, the arguments, in the various perspectives?

You must wonder when I will end this philosophical rambling. These past few years, that is what I miss most about Clayton being gone: discourse, daily conversation which is brimming with meaningful substance. It is my good fortune to have only a few moments each day for such thoughts, high in a tree, surrounded by green leaves, red apples, and a dance of light.

Your Sister,
Abigail

April 4, 1908

Dear Maggie,

Earlier this evening I set up my easel near the river and tried to paint the sky. There was a softness lingering between the branches of the cottonwoods, the kind of stillness that settles over the valley just before the sun stains the horizon. I tried to get it all on the canvas, Maggie, the thin pink line that scratched the horizon, the gray net which spread through the trees. But somehow my paints felt too heavy and the colors, no matter how I mixed them, turned false as soon as

I brushed them over the canvas. Would that I could set it all down, just as I see it. There would be a kind of peace in getting it right.

Before Amy and Everett left last week, I gave Ellen three of my better attempts at painting the sky and the mesa. She had accompanied me on a few of my painting excursions and had completed her own study of the mesa, a nicely proportioned drawing, especially for a child of eleven. As I have told Amy, her daughter exhibits both interest and talent in drawing, which could easily be cultivated. Everett has convinced her that artistic endeavors are frivolous activities, appropriate for filling our leisurely hours, of which there should not be too many. But never mind. Amy is an excellent mother, and as Ellen attends school with your grandchildren, I am sure she is receiving an education which will serve her well in all things.

Last week Teresa broke her arm. The bone was split entirely and protruded through the skin, and so I took her to the nearest doctor, who in turn sent us to a clinic, where her arm was examined under X-ray. I had no idea of the medical advances that have taken place. The doctor used chloroform to put her to sleep while they cut the arm open and wired the bones into place. I have asked her to stay with us, so that I could nurse her more easily, but she will not leave her kitchen, where all of her plants are hung. She applies various poultices throughout the day, and her rapid improvement has been impressive. She knows how to heal even herself.

Paula has left dinner for Anna and me, and after I end this correspondence, I shall heat it. The house Paula and José live in is visible from my front yard, and Anna spends much of her day playing with their four children. Once every few years, Paula hears word of her brother, Ramon. He has remarried and has two small children. They live on his wife's father's ranch in Mexico. Paula hates what he has done, disowning his own child, annulling his first marriage. I sometimes worry she cares for Anna out of penance, but both she and Teresa seem to have a genuine love for the child. Paula treats her like one of her own.

Your Sister,
Abigail

August 6, 1908

Dear Maggie,

Margaret arrived last month. She came by train and had only a trunk with a few dresses in it and a hat, all her worldly possessions. She had been involved with a man, and I still do not know his name or much about him, but I am sure he was not a decent sort. She claimed all kinds of things about him, once that he had become rich by investing in property in California, and that he had taken her with him on expensive automobile trips to San Francisco, buying silk dresses and hats and shoes, even several parasols for her use. She knew of the earthquake but said she was too far east of it to be harmed. I am not sure that the whole story isn't made up. She was not clear why she had left such a situation in haste. I am fairly certain they were never married.

Three weeks after her arrival, I took her to the asylum and had her admitted. Twice she had tried to take her own life, once with Clayton's rifle, and several times she got on a horse and rode off for hours until I was frantic with worry. José took a horse and followed her early one morning, reporting that she rode far out into the hills, following no path that he could see.

Teresa brewed every sort of concoction, but Margaret would not drink of them, complaining they were foul. I don't know that even Teresa's magic could help her. The doctor said he would keep her for several months. They have a problem with overcrowding, and I hated to leave her in such a place; it was dirty and filled with vile smells. But I do not know what else there is for me to do. I keep her in my prayers.

Abigail

October 19, 1908

Dear Maggie,

You write that you "cannot help but find more and more about (my) life outrageous." If I were not your sister you would see much of what has happened as "unacceptable." Do you think that you can change the circumstances of Margaret's insanity by finding it "unacceptable"? I suppose you are also referring to my raising of Anna, my friendships with Paula and Teresa and with Thomas Mayfield. There seems to be much that you criticize me for.

I suppose old age becomes you more. You have a son who will take over the managing of the store and another who plans to run for state senator. Irene has four "lovely children." By your own accounts, you spend your days socializing with the ladies of Stillwater, attending to charities, giving advice to your children, and caring for your grandchildren. Your evenings are spent with John, "quiet evenings in the home, lingering over dinner or reading together." Your life is so good.

I am glad also that Mother never had to know of "her granddaughter locked up in some asylum." It is an illness Margaret has, like any other sickness. She cannot help herself.

Your Sister,

Abigail

December 2, 1908

Dear Maggie,

I have learned of your conspiracy. Did you think you could involve Jenny Alden and she would not tell me. She, at least, has remained my loyal friend. You will never be able to have Anna raised by others because her mother has been declared unfit, at least while I am living. And this threat is reason enough to keep me alive for at least another decade. Amy has written asking forgiveness for her part, but I cannot help thinking that the ill plan was yours from the start; your silence condemns you.

As you know, Amy and Everett plan to visit next month. She has promised to make an effort on Anna's behalf to see her as a niece, a cousin to Ellen. We have had our differences, but I am convinced she meant well and was concerned that my health might fail if the responsibility were too much to carry.

I am not sure I understand your motives as clearly. Would you stretch your hand across these miles that lie between us to take hold of my life? Is it because we have spent so many years apart, because I am a stranger to you ("I cannot," you have written, "understand the circumstances of your life or the decisions you seem moved to make"), that you reach out blindly to try to control my life?

I *remain,*
Abigail

March 29, 1909

Dear Maggie,

I am enclosing your most recent letter. I cannot bear to have it in my possession. Your attitude is similar to the foolishness I have encountered in town. In spreading the news throughout the sewing group that I have no moral backbone, Pamela Porter, who used to be one of my closest friends, has shown herself for what she really is, petty and close-minded. By your letter, I must conclude that you are of the same species. Even if Anna were black like a Negro, I would not allow her to be taken from me.

Margaret was here in October for a brief visit after she was discharged from the asylum. When she left, it was with no clear plans of where she would go next. She talked about traveling south where Anna's father lives, but he has remarried and has more children. Teresa says he has become a bandit and the meanest sort of man. She does not know him for her son. I was relieved to have Margaret go, and I do not expect her to return with any regularity or to help in any way with raising her child. However she might dote on Anna one minute, the next minute she forgets the child exists.

Paula sits outside, pulling the husks from the corn or stringing peppers as she watches the children play. They sometimes spend all morning chasing one another in circles or playing some other game. I enjoy it most when they sing.

Their sounds drift through the house until I feel that I could be in heaven. In truth, they almost never fight with one another, or if they do, Paula hurries them off to her own house, claiming they will hurt the grandmother's ears with their shouting.

I look up from the letter I am writing and see their dark heads now framed by the window, and all around them the blue of the sky. Does it matter into what color skin we are born?

I remain,

Abigail

January 5, 1909

Dear Abigail,

My motives in trying to find a suitable home for your grandchild were to save you from having to take that difficult but inevitable step yourself. You are nearly seventy; who would care for the child if you were to die? Her mother could come at any time and take her. Think of it, poor, senseless Margaret. And then what would become of the child?

I wish you had been able to come for the holidays. Surely winter must be difficult without any relations. Perhaps next year you could come and stay with John and me or Amy for the remainder of the winter. It was a lovely Christmas, with a tree Robert had cut for us, all decorated, and the house trimmed with ribbons and pine cones and lace. They came here to celebrate, all of them, Irene with her husband and four children, Robert and his family. Alex and Susan, who traveled all the way from Baltimore, where she works for the newspaper. And your Amy came with Everett and Ellen. So many grandchildren. I had filled various dishes with candies and spread them about, and there were the candies I had hung on the tree. Oh, they had a time finding them all and were filled with sweets before they left.

Irene and Amy did all the cooking—the turkey and dressing, potatoes, green peas, breads, pudding, the pies. I had nothing but to sit in the armchair with the children playing all around me and take in the smells of the cooking. When they were done and the meal eaten, Amy came to sit by me at the partially empty table, saying she did not know what could be done about Anna, since it was clear you would refuse any help she tried to offer.

I do not know myself and told her so. The child is dark-skinned— Amy says it is—like a Mexican or some Indian, a child of mixed origins with no father who will claim it and a mother who should by all rights have remained committed to an asylum. Who knows what this Anna will do with her life, given her heritage?

It is a difficult thing to watch the family line be extended this way. You have said that Anna's father's mother and sister care for her. Perhaps they or some other member of their family would claim her and take the responsibility of raising her. It would be more simple. Surely you must see it would benefit her also. Think how many minds you would ease if you could agree to some reasonable, some moral resolution.

Yours, in sincerity,
Maggie

Chapter 9

July 7, 1915

Dear Maggie,

Today is my seventy-fifth birthday. When I look back-
wards, I cannot imagine how I have allowed my refusal to write
to you to continue for this long. One thing you must admit,
your tenacity is equal or nearly equal to mine, for it has been
more than five years since I have heard any news of you except
for the bits Amy sends me. Have we become two sullen, foolish
old women that we cannot step beyond what has happened and
forgive one another? This birthday gives me pause, and I realize
I cannot afford to let any more time pass without at least trying
to make amends. I pledge my best effort.

You have no doubt read that we were granted statehood three years ago. Everywhere flags were unfurled in celebration, and I had the good fortune of hearing President Taft speak when he made his tour. It was a long and difficult climb. What a wondrous feeling to wake up a citizen of the state of New Mexico and know that the children born here will have the guarantee of an education.

We were in our third year of drought that fall, and there was nothing to be had, no corn, no milk from the cow. If not for José and our Spanish neighbors, Anna and I would have perished. But we have had rain the past two years, enough to fill the rivers again, and the valley is once again green.

Margaret comes to stay periodically, and each time I see how her illness has progressed. I have taken her to the doctors in the city, and various treatments were recommended, but nothing seems to help her. She has tried to poison herself with quicksilver. There was an asylum they wanted to put her in, but I would not let them. Perhaps I am to blame, trying to raise children in an unsettled place. She is as wild as the sage brush she ran through each day of her childhood, as unpredictable as the jack rabbits she chased. It is George's opinion that if a girl could run cattle, she would have been happy and not harmed herself.

George has settled on a ranch north of here, near the Colorado border. It is a large ranch, to hear him tell of it, but I have never got up there to see it. He is in charge of the entire operation and lives in a small house. I don't know that he will ever marry; he is forty-five years old now and so used to doing for himself, but there is a woman who washes his laundry. Once a year he comes for a visit, and I hardly know him for my son when he slides off his horse, picking me up and swinging me around as if I were a child.

Last month, the day before Margaret left, she spent all afternoon running through the desert until I had to ask José to go and find her, to bring her home. For another hour she screamed at the walls in her room, railing against me, then slept until late morning. That afternoon, when she disappeared without leaving a trace, I put on my riding clothes and rode up to the mesa on the gentle mare George had brought me.

It was a hot afternoon, so hot that I pictured them finding my old-woman bones weeks later, picked clean by buzzards. The sky pulsed with light, and when I looked across the sand I seemed to see small pools of water everywhere reflecting it. A dry, hot wind blew as I sat on my horse before the mesa, its shape cut against the sky, that mesa as familiar as any house to me. My eyes touched every part of it—the small piñons that grow at the base and the dark cedars that push themselves between the crevices, and the purple of the rock, everywhere rock. I leaned back in the saddle Clayton had ridden in and turned my face up to the sky. Its light poured through me, the dry heat.

Somehow, Maggie, I've let go of everyone now—my

littlest children and Clayton, George, Amy, Margaret, many of the friends I made here, and you also, Maggie. It is that each day blows into the next one, all equally filled with light, and I do not expect or even hope for a letter or a visit. It no longer occurs to me to take the train east, where I could stay indefinitely with Amy and her family.

You will probably think this the babbling of an old, mindless woman. No doubt you and John are the contented elderly couple, surrounded by your children and grandchildren and nephews and nieces. Anna is becoming a young woman. My granddaughter, at least, I have not lost. And although I seldom leave the ranch, Thomas Mayfield continues to visit me, and Jenny Alden rode out just last week. Teresa is here, and Paula and José. I would change not anything I have done in my life.

Your Sister,

Abigail

December 14, 1915

Dear Maggie,

I did not write last summer to receive your pity. Please know that I am content with the life I have made for myself. Señora Teresa, with her bags of leaves and the piles of ripe pumpkins and squash she somehow harvested even when no

281

rain fell, is still a great comfort to me, and I am able to attend church, where I see Jenny Alden. Once or twice a month, José drives Anna and me in the wagon. He leaves us by the front door and goes with Paula and their children to the nearby Catholic church. We are the gossip of the morning, but I sit with Anna in the back and do not pay it any mind. During the winter months José drives Anna to school. I twist her hair into pincurls each night and tie it up with ribbons before she leaves. She looks quite the young lady.

Pamela Porter passed away three years ago, but before she died she came to see me. It was during the last year of the drought, and we were two dried husks whispering and finally laughing together over the past. "What does any of it matter?" she said at last, and so we were reconciled.

I have learned to forget my other "Christian" friends who have deserted me. Surely a just God would see nothing "unseemly" or sacrilegious in my life. It is social custom which they are defending, and an unfair one at that. American men constantly make pregnant the "dark beauties," some of whom work in their homes. These men worship the Lord each Sunday, and the ladies of the church turn their heads the other way and do not notice the Mexican or Indian babe with light hair or a pale complexion.

Thomas Mayfield is dead now also. He came out to stay with me late last summer, during the harvest. We spent the days riding up into the mountains and watching José and his sons bring in the corn and beans and bright chile peppers. The dark-green alfalfa was already bundled, so much of it there was, and the trees were heavy with apples, for it had been a good summer, with plenty of rain.

One day we went out into the orchard and picked apples. The ladders are long, and there we were high up in the trees, touching the red fruit, the leaves, and all of that light, light, light, the sky. Bees hummed with the sweetness. "I've found one, Abigail," Thomas called out. "It's perfect. Completely red." And I heard him bite into it, heard him sigh with how deeply he enjoyed it.

Later we brought out chairs and watched the sun set behind the mountains, among the trees, a thick, honey-colored light. And then it was November and he was dead, of a stroke, his daughter told me in the telegram she sent. She came back from the east to prepare for his funeral and asked me to attend.

There was a crowd of people there to mourn him, many of those, I suppose, who had been his patients or read his books on the southwest. I did not know anyone, except for the daughter, whom I had met once. Afterwards she asked that I come the next day to his house, where she was staying while she cleaned it out. The next morning when I arrived she gave me the drawings and paintings I had given to her father over the years and a watercolor which he had made recently, a bright-blue sky filled with leaves and red apples.

"He spoke of you often," she said before I left. "He missed my mother terribly."

I have little reason to travel now to Santa Fe, but last week I rode there in an automobile with Jenny Alden. "Come with me," she had said. "It will do you good." And so we laughed, two old women, for even Jenny is old now, in an auto bumping at that accelerated speed over the dirt roads.

The city is so changed, with electric lights that make the streets glow as soon as the sun goes down, and the theaters, which all advertise moving picture shows. I convinced Jenny that we should go inside one to see what the fuss is about, and so we bought tickets. The story line was rather foolish, but I cannot comprehend how the pictures are made to move across the screen. It is a marvelous invention.

At any rate, I have strayed too long from my purpose in writing, which is to wish you the best of holidays. I would send a greeting card, but as I seldom leave the ranch, I do not have any. This will have to suffice. It is a dark and chilling day, but I am seated in an armchair beside the stove, both dogs curled at my feet. I would make a cozy picture.

Your Sister,
Abigail

June 17, 1916

Dear Maggie,

We have had a beautiful spring, the valley and desert sown with color. The alfalfa fields have turned a deep purpled green and are ready for another cutting. Yesterday morning I walked into the orchard and saw the small apples hanging like ornamental balls in the early sun. I nearly reached up to pick one, they looked so golden in that light.

I read in the newspapers of the fighting in Europe. There is talk of sending our troops. If we enter the war, will they send for your grandsons? I believe George, at forty-six, is too old. He has numerous injuries from cattle ranging, so that I cannot imagine they would take him.

I did enjoy seeing Amy and Everett last month. It was so good of Ellen to take time off her studies at the university to accompany them. It had been three years since I had seen her, and I was impressed at what an attractive, articulate young woman she has become. Amy is fifty-three years now, I cannot believe it, and Everett is nearly sixty. He was suffering with a sore back while they were here, so Ellen and I and Anna went out riding without them.

"Watch out for your grandmother," Amy called to Anna and her daughter as we got on the horses. She does not seem to comprehend that I ride out alone still as often as I like when they are not here. I stayed back and let those two young women take the lead out across the desert and along the base of the mountains. I heard their laughter and pieces of their conversation. It was good to see them together this way.

Bea Manning was here in April for a few weeks, after all the years it has been. She was traveling by railroad to Colorado, to stay with her son. Oh, it did me good to see her. We two went riding along the river and up into the mountains. She does not seem nearly as old as I am, for her skin is soft and her hair is still nearly all dark. This she attributes to her lack of association with men the past forty years. "They age us, Abigail," she told me.

I do not think she is right. Teresa says it is the desert air that has carved deep lines into our faces. Her wrinkled skin has softened these past few years, so that it is nearly translucent. She looks as if she has come from another world. Indeed, when she stares at me with her dark, clear eyes and speaks what is in my heart, I think she has already stepped part way into the life that lies beyond this one.

Your Sister,
Abigail

September 3, 1917

Dear Maggie,

I send my condolences on John's death. It was a long and blessed life the two of you had together. You must rest easier knowing he is no longer in pain and that he is peacefully awaiting your reunion. You said an old woman should not grieve, but I do not think you are right about this. Grief has grown next to contentment in my life, twisting together like vines that feed on one another, their wide leaves climbing towards the sky. I do not know if it is possible to have one without the other.

You write that two of your grandsons are overseas fighting the war and could not come for John's funeral. I will pray for them, as I have read in the newspapers how many are being killed. Teresa's grandson died in the fighting. She brought me the papers that say this is true, but neither of us can understand it, how this happened. There was no body to bury. Such a war as they say it is must be terrible. The newspapers are full of what the Germans have done, and I suppose it is right to hate them.

A small orange tree grows in my kitchen. The bright balls hang from the smooth dark leaves, and I think every morning it is like summer to have a bit of color in the house, a piece of brightness. I wander about from window to window and look out upon the desert I have lived my life upon. Each day it is new. I am no closer to knowing it than when

I rode across it for the first time, a young woman in a covered wagon.

Your Sister,

Abigail

October 19, 1918

Dearest Maggie,

Every morning I walk along the river where the cottonwoods have turned to yellow and the river bed is nearly dry. The muddy water moves slowly downstream. There is a young oak tree, and it is all red brilliance under the wide blue sky. Sometimes I think that is why I have stayed these many years, Maggie, and not been able to make myself leave—the color, the color, oh, the color. Picture an azure sky and the red oak and yellow cottonwood leaves flashing against it. I could sit and stare into them all morning, and some days I do just that. If Anna sees me sitting against a tree close to the bank, she carries me a sweater and a blanket to sit on, even if it is quite warm.

I am sorry for the loss of your grandson Michael. Amy has written that he was killed in France. Irene, she writes, is nearly mad with the loss. Will Steven be sent home? Surely the loss of one son is enough for anyone to give to such a war.

Your Sister,

Abigail

April 26, 1920

Dear Maggie,

Today is Anna's wedding day. It is early in the morning, just before sunrise, and I should waken her and begin the preparations, but as I woke, the thought was there that I hadn't written to you in so long, that I hadn't told you she was being married. Maggie, I forget now; sometimes whole days slip by. I know somewhere I have a letter from you, unanswered.

Amy and Ellen arrived yesterday, and Amy says she has told you of the wedding but that I should write down the details. Anna is to marry José and Paula's oldest son, Tadeo. "He is too much like a brother," I have told her, for indeed they are cousins. But since her father never claimed her, no one else but me finds fault with the match. It will make inheritance of the land favorable, for the two of them, they shall have it all.

Two weeks now Paula has spent baking and cooking, following her mother's recipes for *cabrito* and carne con chile and all sorts of breads and fruit pies. Teresa walks about the kitchen fussing that the dough has not risen enough, the lamb is not tender. George wrote that he would arrive this morning. He can spare only two days for the trip. Today I will sit in their church, the one with the painted statues, next to Teresa. I'll watch Anna walk to the altar in the dress

Paula and I have sewn for her. They all call her Anita, and she prefers it. But I cannot. She will always be my Anna.

Your Sister,

Abigail

June 17, 1922

Dear Maggie,

This morning I climbed into the mountains, higher than I have gone these past ten years. I was following a small herd of mountain sheep. They were like ghosts, Maggie, desert spirits wandering through the heat, eating what was saturated with light. "Come, little one," I called to the smallest, and she let me reach my hand out to brush her cloud-like hair.

I do not know how I could wander forgetting the time and which paths I had taken, but I did forget while following the small, white herd. It was nearly noon and the sun high in the sky when I realized I was lost. Twice I turned around in the hot sun, and the sheep disappeared, as if their gray shapes had melted into the muted colors of sage brush and clay, their thick horns hardened to rock.

I was at first frightened when I realized I had lost my way, for I had only a little water with me. But then my sight cleared, and I saw for the first time a fine weave of threads that ran from bush to rock to tree, disappearing as they stretched toward sky. I saw how the threads touched me, the bright cords nearly invisible but so tightly coiled their strands could not be pulled apart.

And now that I am home again, having found my way somehow through the light and heat, I cannot imagine what it was I saw. I remember only the brightness of it. Teresa says it is like Saint Francis to be led by the spirit of an animal. Anna is certain it was heat stroke. She has sworn she will tell Amy, who is to visit next month, of my mishap, and I am to be followed if I venture again up into the mountains, like the old fool I suppose I have become.

Are you, too, old, Maggie? This old? I cannot understand how it has happened.

Your Sister,
Abigail

March 2, 1925

Dear Maggie,

This morning I finished my final painting of the mesa. My eyesight has failed these last months, but it seemed to reappear, unaltered, long minutes at a time while I finished my painting. And oh, Maggie, now that I cannot see the colors of the world, I find they are fixed inside my mind so that I see them always, brilliant as ever they were. Strange that when I could no longer see the mesa, I finally understood how to paint it.

Maggie, I would send these paintings to you. I have wrapped them in paper and tried to puzzle out where to take them so that they can be safely sent. The railroad, I suppose, is obvious, but the problem is I no longer travel off this land. If I can see my way clear to it, I will have Anna carry them there for me.

Maggie, I am not sure why, but after all these years I want you to have the world I have seen. Perhaps it is because I still want confirmation that this strange land was worth losing you and the life I would have had in Virginia. I pray that I will find the proper means to deliver them.

Abigail

November 12, 1927

Dear Maggie,

I rode in a wagon today, up into the mountains to gather the piñons. Anna has a husband and three children, all brown as clay, and I am asked, the grandmother, the old, white-haired woman, to accompany them. And what does it matter, my skin so wrinkled it could be any color?

So many nuts falling from the trees, the sweet smell all through the air and ground. The children scooping handfuls and dancing. We filled the wagon all morning, it seemed, while from the tops of the trees a long, thin cry circled. "A place of ghosts," Anna called out, or was it Teresa, who has left me finally to be the old one alone. They say she ran out into the field when it was covered with butterflies and that she gathered them in her wide skirt and flew into the air. She would have laughed. I can hear her still. Now I am the bruja, the old woman they whisper of, with my handful of salt and charcoal.

"Coyotes," I told myself when the sound came again, their cries like death. And: "Clayton will go and fire his rifle." Too many I think of now are gone, my Jenny and Paula. Margaret is here and then not here. Anna tells me George visited the entire month of September. How could I have forgotten? If I could, I would straighten time so that it runs like a river bed.

Your Sister,
Abigail

May 27, 1930

My Dear Maggie,

I saw the sun come up this morning, turning the desert red. Now I sit on the front porch looking out over my yard, where the prickly pear blossoms a deep pink. I seem to have fallen asleep and dreamed for a few moments that I was a young girl again in Virginia, where the yard was a lush green and we two were running across it, our skirts filling with the wind. You stopped at the line of trees and held your hands out to me, and when I took them, we danced perfectly in step with one another.

Forgive me, dear Maggie, for not writing to you these many years, but as Anna says, I am an old woman and forget much of the time to do as I should. Perhaps I will come east for a visit. Amy says I must and soon. She promised to take the train west, to come and see me, but then poor Everett broke his leg. I have great-grandchildren there now, for Anna tells me that Ellen married some five or six years ago. I cannot remember their names. These days my body has wings and the world I touch is sky, sky, sky.

Your Sister,
Abigail

Epilogue

Last month, shortly after I signed the papers for Anita's land six months after her death, I began to clean the closets and attics of everything left there, old or unused. In the crawl space over the older section of the house, where a bird startled into dark, dusty flight, I found a large package wrapped in stiff brown paper, the address written in familiar script: Mrs. Margaret Mason, 175 Vine Street, Stillwater, Virginia.

Julia helped me to peel away the paper, and we found three canvases dated during the last years of Abigail's life, thick with explosions of color, heavy brush strokes of red, brown, purple spreading out of blues, as if the landscape was set in motion by the sky. My grandmother had two of Abigail's paintings in her house, but they were more realistic desert landscapes, carefully proportioning the land to the sky or detailing the borders of a ridge. Their colors and strokes were highly controlled, almost artificial. These three paintings, done at the end of Abigail's life, broke loose of all form, so that the mesa was unrecognizable, and it was impossible to tell where the sky ended. When I looked at them, I experienced the same feeling I had when gazing off towards the mountains or looking across the sweep of valley: I was lost in the raw sensation of color and space.

I hung Abigail's paintings on the wall in the living room, across from the window that looks out towards the mountains and the long flat mesa. In the late afternoon, as the world's colors deepen, they are like strange mirrors, reflecting what the eye takes apart, the image it keeps in memory.

A few months after coming to New Mexico, I moved in with Anita and Julia. The first winter I learned to make tamales, spreading corn husks with *masa* and *chile*, folding the husks and steaming them until their smell filled the house. The three of us baked *bollitos* and *molletes*, we cooked large pots of tomatoes and garlic and peppers, and while everything simmered and roasted and baked, I read Abigail's letters. By spring, when I looked out across the old orchard or the fields where the mesa rose nearly symmetrical in the distance, I saw her history layered there, the words she had written crisscrossed like a bright net laid over the world.

That first year I met the others who live on the same road: Hernandos, who had moved back to the valley after working for three years in the city; Cheryl, a retired nurse; Carol and Mark, who had moved from Denver to farm the land; and David, a free-lance photographer, who had returned to the valley where he spent summers with his grandfather while growing up. Through them I have become involved in a struggle to prevent the state from damming the river to provide more water for the nearby city, which is rapidly expanding. We've written articles and taken photographs, hoping to save the valley, with its small farms and orchards, from being put under water or turned back to desert.

At first I tried to retrieve the farmland, planting a field of alfalfa, irrigating the orchard and transplanting more saplings. I carefully designed a large vegetable garden. But I knew little about farming, and even with Anita's advice, I let in too much water from the acequia or planted the seeds too close to the soil's surface or forgot to account for the long dry months of June and July. I now work part time as a substitute teacher at the high school. I have given up cultivation, except for tending a small vegetable and flower garden next to the house, but I still spend much of my time outside, walking along the river or climbing up into the desert or chasing Julia across the yard. In the evenings I often meet with my neighbors to work on saving the valley.

Anita must have already suffered several small strokes before I came that first time to see her. The morning I drove her to a nearby hospital after finding her semiconscious on the kitchen floor, she warned me to be careful that I didn't drive over any small animals. She was especially worried about the tiny lizards that she kept seeing dart out between shadows or from the mirages of pooled water. "Slower," she kept insisting, until I was afraid she would try to make me pull over and let her out to walk the long way through the desert heat.

There was not much they could do for her at the hospital, and she refused to take the medicines they prescribed, boiling roots for herself instead. As the year went on, she had more difficulty walking and began mistaking me for her daughter. Some days she did not speak at all, and one winter evening she flung open the door, calling to her mother, whom she was sure she had seen bent over on a horse, riding across the field. "Her hair was still dark," she marveled later. "All undone in the wind."

She seldom talked about Abigail. Once she told me her grandmother had continued to sew a dress for her each year, even after she was married and had children of her own. The stitches Abigail made by hand were as tiny and even as those made on a machine. Another story she told about her grandmother was how she had carried her up into the mountains in a wagon when her grandmother could no longer walk. "My grandmother begged me, and so I made a bed of quilts and pillows, and all morning we rode until we reached the top of the mesa. Then I had to wake her so that she could look out across the sky at the valley below."

Anita's sons had both moved to the city some years before with their families. They came to visit on occasional weekends, clearly puzzled by my presence, the crazy easterner with some exaggerated claim of being a relative. At first they wanted me to leave, but later, confused and then relieved by Anita's and Julia's growing dependence on me, they seemed to accept that I had come to stay.

That second spring after I came to New Mexico, Anita took me up into the mountains to see the place where the river separated to create the valley below. She had learned from her neighbors of the plan to build a dam there and wanted to show me the source of the valley's water, the place where the dam would be constructed.

It was a spot high up in the mountains, along the same ridgeline that cut into the mesa. Abigail, I knew, would have ridden to this spot on a horse, but we drove as far as the roads would allow and then got out and began to hike, following the dried ditches and old stream beds that led to the river.

We were silent while hiking. I could not picture the land we walked on under a reservoir of water. Part of the valley also would be flooded, and the rest would become a desert. Anita slid down the deeply grooved path and waited for me to follow with Julia. "They take what they want," she said. I was also afraid that somehow the government would be able to take away the valley.

That afternoon we had walked the two-mile trail that led to the river, when clouds began to blossom across the wide sky, thick cottony white clouds followed by long strings of darker ones. "We should climb back to the car," I yelled down to Anita as I stood with her granddaughter above the wide, swift river, which was the color of iron, a darker gray than the color the sky had turned. Anita slid precariously close to the water's edge in her thick, dark skirts as I yelled again: "A storm's coming."

Finally, I convinced her to climb back up the path to the road where we'd left my car. But the dried-up streams were steeper than I had realized when we'd slid down them and hard to negotiate with a child and an old woman. Anita kept sitting down to rest, her skirts spread out around her, telling me to go on ahead, and Julia was tired by now and crying to be carried. The dried streams were full of stones, and they slid out from under my shoes so that I was pulled back down towards the river. My foot turned in the deep crevices, and twice I painfully twisted my ankle.

When lightning began to streak across the sky above us, I tried to get Anita to climb up out of the dried stream and walk on the higher ground, which was thick with brush, but there were so many cacti, with their long thorns, that we turned back. The rain hit all at once. I remember gripping Julia's hand and pulling her with all my strength from the sudden water. When I held her beside me, high up on the crumbling bank as I could manage to climb, I looked down through the heavy rain and saw Anita, standing already knee deep in foaming water, her face turned into it as if she could see past the pounding torrent to what somewhere must have been the same turquoise sky that had stretched over the world most of her life.

I nearly looked myself to see what was there beyond water, what light, what luminous rim of sky. "Anita," I called to her, and "Anita, Anita, Anita," until she twisted her body slowly towards the bank, her body bent, face full of confusion. "Come towards me and I'll pull you up."

The clay bank was slick by now, partly washed away. After pushing Julia to higher ground, I slid down, hoping Anita would not turn from me in all that water, that she would know to move towards the bank.

But she was already wading back down the dried stream, the way we had come. "Anita." I tried the name over and over. I thought I saw her pause for a moment, hesitating before leaning back into the rain. And then I couldn't find her in all that wilderness of water.

Julia was where I had left her, curled beside the small tree, and I took her higher to wait under what shelter we could find among the rocks. When the storm ended, I would carry her along the top of the river, searching for her grand-mother. But it would be three days before they would find Anita's body downstream, washed to the bank of the river that eventually ran through her land.

I've asked myself many times why I agreed to take an old woman and a child down a steep mountainside, why I didn't realize that a storm could come with such speed. Sometimes I think that I was too much in awe of her, for I was so sure she knew the desert and the mountains and the valley, I believed she was strong and brave enough to keep us from any storm. But perhaps, I tell myself, she wanted to be taken that way, by the land and sky, instead of some sudden flash of light that would come from inside her.

I have lived in New Mexico for three years now. Julia is six years old, a quiet child who knows how to roast chiles and bake *bollitos* and sing with the wind that comes across the desert. In the summer she likes to plant flowers and tomatoes and peppers. She likes to pick fruit with me, climb-ing up into trees thick with the sky that mixes with the green leaves. And she likes to draw with markers or paint with temperas on the large sheets of paper I lay out for her. When she is older, I will read Abigail's letters to her and try to explain how they are tied to the story of how I became her mother.

There are missing pieces to the story told in the letters. Before she died, Anita told me that her mother had returned in 1932, two years after Abigail's death, and had stayed with Anita until she died. Margaret was underweight, with gray skin and sunken cheeks, older looking than her sixty-seven years, and no one could understand how she had been able to survive the trip to the valley. She had been living in Mexico for a number of years, but beyond this Anita knew nothing of where her mother had lived or whom she had lived with or how she had made her living.

For nearly two years, Margaret wandered about the house, sometimes most of the night, in her sleep. During the day, she slept or sat in a chair, talking, singing, laughing. She would become suddenly lucid, telling of a lover who had abused her or a dress that needed mending. Anita's children feared her as if she were a ghost.

When Margaret died, they buried her in the family burial plot near the river, under the tall cottonwoods. I have seen the plot with the markers for Clayton and Abigail, Patricia and Margaret. There is a small stone with no name, which I believe marks the grave of the baby Abigail lost. When Anita died she was buried beside her husband in the graveyard next to the Catholic church.

I've asked my grandmother what happened to George. About the year 1920, George bought a small ranch in northern New Mexico. My grandmother believed he kept a small herd of cattle and had a couple of younger ranch hands that worked for him. Fifteen years later, my grandmother's mother,

Amy, learned that George had disappeared one summer afternoon. No one was sure where he had gone. A ranch hand
said that George had ridden out during a drought to see that
the herd had enough water and had never come back. There
were rumors that he had ridden off into the hills, that he
had been sick, that he had simply disappeared in the hot,
dry air, become one with the dull, flesh-colored landscape.

Not as much land exists around the house anymore, as
Abigail sold some of it, and Anita gave away whatever her
children or her husband's brothers and sisters asked for. But
there is still a garden behind the house, and I've replanted
the bougainvillea and the verbena and hibiscus.

In the mornings and evenings I like to walk with Julia
along the river that runs close to our house, and often we
climb up into the mountains and look out at the horizon,
where the sky draws a darker line against the land. I remind
myself that time is not like light that fills the wide sky. It
is more like water, which can dwindle to a thin stream, then
overflow, gushing madly, and it can be cut off now that we
have the technology to try to control it.

This many years after Abigail's death, parts of the landscape still remain unchanged. From the house I can look out
the window and see Abigail's mesa. Some nights, at the edge
of sleep, I tell myself that in the morning I will once more
ride out to see it.

MAR 1 5 1996

WITHDRAWN